CW00821202

Books in the Series

Twice Told Tales

Lesbian Retellings

Caged Bird Rising by Nino Delia

The Secret of Sleepy Hollow by Andi Marquette
(Coming: October 2015)

Caged Bird Rising

A Grim Tale of Women, Wolves, and Other Beasts

Nino Delia

Ylva

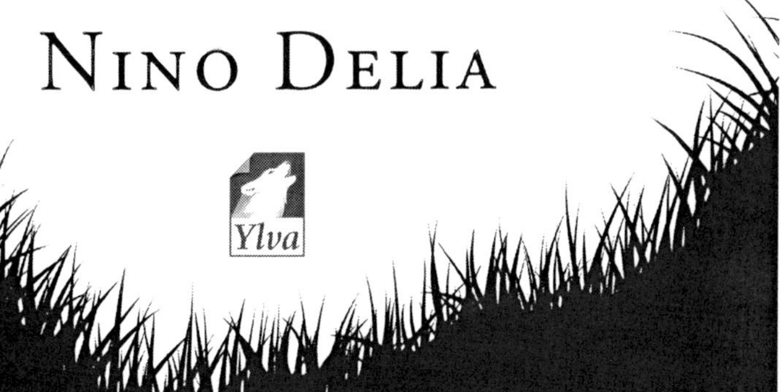

Dedication

For Hanni and Karli.

Acknowledgment

First of all, I want to thank my girl who was always on my tail, urging me to go on.

Anne deserves credit for her pictures, the supportive words, and generally for being my best friend.

Astrid for believing in the power of fairy-tales, and Gill, who did a fantastic job. Without these women, the manuscript would never have come between that splendid cover.

Chapter 1

Once upon a time there was a maiden, fair and chaste, who lived in a small village bordering the oldest forest in the kingdom. Though she was a girl born in times of hunger, her father, a kindhearted man, had not fulfilled his patriarchal duty toward her. Instead, he let her live and even gave her a name.

"Robyn. You're late again!" Granny called from the foot of the stairs.

"I'll be right down." Robyn grabbed her bodice and ran.

"If a man had raised you, you'd have been up before sunrise to start on your chores," Granny scolded. "Instead you're running around like an untrained puppy. What would your father say?"

Granny didn't mean to be harsh—she was old and grouchy—but Robyn always felt sad when she mentioned her father. He had died when she was very young. All she knew was that a dangerous beast had killed him on the dark forest roads. Robyn was lucky Granny had been there to look after her. The old woman grumbled about everything, but she did love Robyn and had done her best to raise her charge right.

"Fetch me the brush." Granny was impatient. "We'll see if I can make that red devil hair of yours respectable for the marketplace."

Robyn handed over the brush. Granny's hands were stiff with arthritis and her brushstrokes tugged at the tangles, but Robyn suffered in silence like a good girl.

"I always did my best to serve your poor departed father." Granny sighed, and her brushstrokes slowed into a rhythm with her memories. "He was a good man. And I do my best by you, too, young lady. Though it would have been so much easier with a man in the house to protect and guide us."

"Granny, you know how much the villagers respect you for being such an excellent surrogate mother," Robyn answered by rote. This was a conversation they often had. Robyn knew the right things to say.

Wrinkled fingers patted her shoulder. "They don't trust me. And they are right not to. A young girl like you needs a strong man to shield you from the evils of the world, not an old crone, like me." It was her favorite lament. Her grandmother had been trained to be an exceptional wife and mother, and that alone kept the villagers from questioning Robyn's upbringing. It helped that Granny had snared a fine young husband for her beautiful granddaughter. A good betrothal was only to be expected for a well-reared girl.

"Thank heavens you have finally filled out," she said. "A girl needs good hips and breasts for nursing her children. Men have an eye for these things." Granny gave her a playful slap on the backside with the brush. "At least you have some qualities for your future husband to look forward to, eh?"

Robyn smiled and handed Granny some hairpins. Granny was a wise woman. Robyn was blessed to be raised by her. "I wouldn't know what to look for in a suitable beau," she confessed.

"That's why I took care of it," Granny said, pinning up Robyn's hair. "You'll know what makes a good man now."

By Granny's standards, Robyn knew that a future husband should be a man of authority. He should have a deep, rich voice to make his wife listen to him. He also had to provide well for his family so his wife could concentrate only on serving his household and raising his children.

Captain Hunter Wolfmounter stepped out of the Red Rider headquarters and headed for the market square. He barely took two steps when Rump Spindlefinger, the richest imp in town, crossed his path.

"Hello, Spindlefinger," Hunter said. "What brings you to market this early in the day?" Spindlefinger's inn never opened before midday. He was usually doing his accountancy in the mornings to make sure not one coin was missing.

"I was helping my wife get the retail wagon into position," Spindlefinger smiled, showing off his rows of gold teeth.

As Captain of the Red Riders, Hunter knew that Spindlefinger had applied for the booth license for this new wagon. Rump Spindlefinger wanted the world to know how well his business was doing. "I hope my new wife will be as hard working as yours."

"Believe me, it wasn't easy, but schooling Robyn should be a simple task for a man like you, Captain," Spindlefinger said. "After all, you will be the first man to train her."

Spindlefinger's usual over-confidence made it sound like an easy task, but Captain Wolfmounter knew better than to underestimate the challenge an unbroken female presented.

"Yes." He nodded. "With no father or brother before me, she will be weak and make many mistakes. As her husband, I will have to teach her how to be a good wife and mother." He was the best man for the job, and he knew it, the same way he had been the best man to lead the Red Riders.

Decades before his birth, wolves began to repopulate the royal forest. Soon the decent people of the kingdom avoided the woods altogether. They were frightened by the wolves and of the thieving scum who lived there, too. Terrified villagers demanded protection, so the King ordered a special patrol be created, the Red Riders, so called because of their red hoods. Every village and town had their own patrol made up of their ablest men. The Red Riders marched through the streets and combed the forest under the King's orders to exterminate evil wherever they found it. Soon enough the forests and mountain roads became safer because of them.

"You know, the best way with women is to give them children as soon as possible. Lots and lots of children." Spindlefinger winked at him. "With any luck she'll be a fertile little thing and pop babies out one right after the other."

Wolfmounter laughed and slapped Spindlefinger on the back. “I’ll see to it, but first we must celebrate our wedding at your inn, my good fellow.”

He bade Spindlefinger farewell and headed for the well in the middle of the market square. His men were already gathered there, waiting for their captain to give them their orders for the day.

“Morning, men.”

“Good morning, sir.” They saluted in unison, standing to attention before him, a bright row of about twenty red cloaks billowing in the wind.

“This is the last of the winter markets, so chances are there’s more than a dozen thieves lurking among our good, honest citizens. I want extra patrols around the booths and on the side streets. The North gate needs no sentry today. Snow has already closed the northern trade route, and no one will be coming that way until the spring thaw.”

His men listened to him intently, and he bathed in their respect before sending them off to work. This was exactly what he wanted from his betrothed. Respect and obedience. He was a good catch for any young woman, and was prepared to be father and husband combined for her. He would show her how good life could be for the dutiful and conscientious wife of the captain.

“Go straight to the market and buy exactly what I told you to,” Granny instructed for the umpteenth time.

Robyn held on to the banister while her grandmother pulled her bodice laces tighter. “You’ve been eating too much pie lately," Granny grumbled, her old fingers struggling with the ties. Although Robyn was betrothed, there was no reason to let her looks go so soon. On the contrary, Granny told her she had to try even harder to look beautiful. Her cheeks needed to be that little bit rosier, and her hair must shine brighter than ever to keep the attentions of her handsome captain. She had to show the village how happy she was to have caught him. She would be a married woman soon, and everyone expected her to be overjoyed to finally have a purpose in her life.

"Buy the yellow potatoes, the good ones. And taste the apples, girl. The ones you brought back last time were bitter." Granny pulled Robyn's green woolen cape over her shoulders. "Remember, you're cooking dinner tonight for the workmen. I'm happy to supervise, but it's your chance to show off your skills. So, buy the best ingredients and fill their bellies well, so they talk about it for days. If you don't, tongues will wag that the Captain's making a mistake, and you're not worthy of his name."

Workmen had fixed the roof on Granny's cottage before the first snow arrived. Robyn could smell the chill of it on the air, moving down from the north. Granny was rewarding their kindness with a dinner. It would stretch their meager rations, but Granny would not accept charity. The men had mended the roof, and Granny and Robyn would repay them as best they could with a good meal.

Robyn had considered going up on the roof herself if only to assess the damage, but Granny nearly fainted at the thought of such behavior in a young woman. What would the villagers think? God forbid Hunter break off his betrothal to such an unnatural girl. Robyn wished she'd never said a word to Granny. What did she know about roofs? As a female, it wasn't her place to repair houses, so she did as she was told and went to politely ask the men for help.

"Yes, Granny, I will only buy the best." She fastened her cape around her neck and kissed her grandmother goodbye. She had to get to market early to get the best bargains. The road to the market square was long and winding, the stones still slippery from the early morning dew. Though her feet hurried, Robyn's thoughts took their time. She worried what would become of her grandmother when she was married and gone to live at Hunter's house. She decided Granny would do exactly what the villagers expected of her. She would take care of the motherless children while their fathers were away working, and she would cook for those same widowers when they came back home. An old woman would always be of use in a village such as this. And when there wasn't a requirement for her services anymore, she would quietly trudge off into the deep woods and disappear, leaving room for a new generation.

Robyn arrived at the market shortly after the booths opened and had the luxury of leisurely browsing the wares on display. Unlike Ebony, who hurried past her already on her way back home. Ebony was the only girl in a large family of boys who all worked at the glass factory, and Ebony had to prepare a huge meal for her seven brothers every night of the week.

Robyn knew she was also luckier than little Ash, who had to bargain with the merchant over the price of lentils, because her father did not take enough care of his wife and family. No, Robyn was glad she would soon be Hunter's wife. He was handsome and strong and had a decent income. She would never have to worry about feeding and clothing their children.

"Good morning, Goldie." Robyn went over to visit her friend who was sitting at her spinning wheel.

"Robyn, why are you out this early?" Goldie brushed her hands on her apron then reached under her stall to retrieve a small package. "Here is the linen your grandmother ordered. Give me six shillings and we're good."

"Six? Only six?" Robyn raised a brow. Linen cost almost double that when she bought it from Spindlefinger, Goldie's husband.

Goldie looked away. "It's an old order that was never collected. It's perfect, it even has the Spindlefinger monogram embroidered in gold thread. It's old stock, but there's no difference in quality."

Robyn opened the package and stroked the monogram. "Thank you for saving me money." Robyn handed over her shillings and put the linen into her basket. "I mustn't let Granny know, though. The leftover money will be useful when I'm married."

"How so?" Goldie looked at her.

Robyn leaned forward so as not to be overheard. "This means I'll have a little extra on top of what Hunter gives me for housekeeping. I can go and buy the best meat and the bigger potatoes, and he'll praise me for handling his money so well."

Goldie gasped and shook her head. "You cannot lie to him," she whispered. "What if you run out of money? You will be forced to buy the ordinary things and he will think you stopped caring."

Robyn bit her lip; she hadn't thought about that. She must never give her husband a reason to think ill of her; that was Granny's very first lesson. Goldie put a hand on her arm and smiled. "Why don't you buy him a wedding gift with it? Better yet, show him your jar of shillings after the wedding. Think how proud he'll be to see you saving money so responsibly."

Robyn clapped her hands in happiness at that and thanked Goldie for her advice. A proud husband would be a wonderful start into her new life as the wife of Hunter Wolfmounter.

A large hand wrapped around her shoulder and startled her. "My lovely," Hunter said. "What a pleasure to see you." It was as if their talk had conjured him up.

Before Robyn and Goldie could say goodbye, he pulled her away. Her skin itched where his hand rested on her shoulder.

"I hope you had a good morning. Mine has certainly improved since seeing you," he said, leading them into the heart of the market.

Robyn smiled, happy with the compliment. "Granny sent me to buy the ingredients for tonight's dinner. I hope you'll be able to come."

"Of course, I could never miss the chance of spending an evening with you. Unfortunately, I'm on duty later, so I'll have to leave early."

"You will be careful, won't you?" She feared for him when he went on patrol, as was to be expected for one's brave betrothed.

"My dear." He sighed and stroked her cheek. "Don't worry about me. I know how to keep myself safe."

"Of course you do, or else you would never have slain the beast and become captain of the Red Riders." She tried to sound proud of his accomplishments.

"As soon as we are married, you will be known as the woman who tamed the most handsome wolf in the valley. Our boys will be little wolf cubs running around your skirts." He bared his teeth and growled playfully. She ducked her head and giggled as he kissed her throat, growling as if he really were a wolf catching his prey. He stroked her hair and kissed her forehead. Then, checking that no one was looking, he gave her his best shiny smile as his hand slid under her cape to pinch her bottom. "Until tonight, lovely."

He turned and left. Robyn watched him go. What a man. And soon she would be his. A small ache nestled in her stomach, but she ignored it as she always did.

Hunter had kept her back so Robyn had to hurry to finish her shopping. She gathered her basket and wandered over to see Whitney and Rose. The twins were the daughters of Darwin Prospector, a sullen old widower who was the foreman at the glass factory. His wife had landed him with female twins before dying on him. Such was his fear of it happening again, he had never remarried.

"How is your father?" Robyn asked. Darwin's health was not working to his benefit anymore.

"Cranky as always." Rose shrugged.

Her sister poked her in the arm. "Don't say that. Father works long hours to put food onto the table."

Rose rolled her eyes and gestured around the stall. "We work long hours, too. We grow and sell all our own produce. It takes hard work to grow herbs and vegetables this tasty," Rose said. "And we cook all the damn food he sets on the table anyway."

Rose was never one for holding back. The village was used to her brazen talk, and that was the reason she was not married. Who wanted a woman who talked back when there were so many other girls willing to be a quiet, obedient little wife? Whitney had it the hardest, though. No man would look twice at her because of her loud, rebellious sister. What if, once married, Whitney became the same? Or worse still, her children turned out as unruly and difficult as their aunt Rose?

"Anyway," Rose said. "How can we help you?"

Robyn looked over the display on the table. "I need parsley and sage."

"For the big dinner tonight?" Whitney asked. "I heard it's for the workmen who repaired your roof." News traveled fast in the small village.

Robyn went to answer, but Rose was faster. "Of course it is, silly. Father will be there, too, stuffing his fat belly, while we sit by the hearth waiting for him like the good little daughters we are."

Robyn was shocked; she would never speak out like Rose did. Darwin Prospector was a widower and would always need one of his daughters to take care of him. He sometimes went to other villages, where nobody knew about Rose, and bragged about Whitney, his pretty, good-natured daughter who was available for marriage. If one day Whitney married and moved away he would always have Rose as his caretaker, and Rose knew it. She was trapped, and that made her angry, Robyn supposed.

"We don't have any sage today," Rose said, wrapping the parsley in a thin strip of sackcloth.

"No sage!" Granny had given her precise instructions. Sage was an important ingredient for the main course. She had to impress the menfolk with her meal, most of all Hunter. "But I need sage."

Rose and Whitney had the only booth that sold herbs. It was too late to try the next village. She should have ordered everything days ago like Granny told her to. She had failed at the first and simplest hurdle, buying the basic dinner ingredients!

"It's too cold to grow sage in our garden, but you might find some growing wild in the woods," Rose suggested. "Everything holds out a little longer there; the trees shelter the earth, so it stays warmer longer."

Whitney was aghast. "Don't tell her to do that!" she said. "The beasts will get her."

Rose rolled her eyes. "She doesn't have to go far into the forest to find wild sage." She turned to Robyn, ignoring her sister's protests. "I go there when our stock gets low."

Whitney looked horrified. "Watch what you say." She hissed. "We're meant to sell only homegrown herbs, not the wild stuff."

Robyn didn't care whether the herbs were wild or homegrown. She needed sage and she didn't care where it came from. Rose explained exactly where she had to go to find the wild sage bushes growing in the forest.

Robyn paid for the parsley and hurried away. She still had to finish her shopping, but at least she knew where to find her last, elusive herb.

It should take her no time at all.

Chapter 2

It took much longer than Robyn thought to finish her shopping. Finally, she made her way homeward to Granny's cottage but she did not go straight there. Instead, at the far end of the village she turned toward the woods.

A cold wind snapped her cloak around her legs, and the shadows grew longer as the weak winter sun began to set, even though the noon hour had barely past. She had to hurry, she dared not stay out after dark, that's when the evil creatures, both man and animal, emerged. Near the edge of the village, outside the walls where the farmers lived, the houses began to thin out. People did not build their homes this close to the forest, and soon she was walking alone along the path. The North gate was unguarded, so she had no trouble slipping through it and walking quickly across the grass.

Soon the edge of the forest was before her. The trade route had been closed only a few weeks and already the narrow path was overgrown. It happened eerily fast, she thought. From the South gate, the path was wide and dry. There, the pumpkin fields opened up on either side of the road, and the sun hung on the horizon allowing the farmers wives a longer working day. On the north side, the dense treetop canopy stopped sunlight drying out the ground, so everything felt damp and dull. Robyn's breath clouded in the chill air as she left the path and stepped into the forest, hitching up her skirt and pushing on through the undergrowth where the air smelled of wet earth and leaf mold.

She carefully stepped over tree roots and slippery moss-covered rocks. She was frightened. The quiet gloominess was overwhelming. Not even a bird sang. Her breath became shallow and her chest tight, but she kept moving deeper into the trees, focusing on the plants, searching for sage. Rose had said she wouldn't need to go very far to find some, but Robyn couldn't see any. If she arrived home late her grandmother would be angry, but if she came home without the herb it would be even worse. Even though the men might not taste the difference, she would know about her failure.

A twig snapped behind her. She spun around with hammering heart, but there was nothing. Torn between feeling both terrified and foolish she glared hard into the gloom until she was certain she was alone, then she turned back.

"Hello, lovely, what are you doing here?" Hunter stood before her, so close her nose was almost buried in his chest. She stifled a scream and stepped back. How had he crept up so quietly?

He put his hands on her shoulders and shook her more forcefully than was playful.

"The sun has almost set. Soon it will be dangerous for a little girl like you to be out. Why didn't you go straight home from the market?"

"How did you find me?" she asked.

He let out an exasperated sigh. "One of the Prospector girls was worried you'd gone into the woods looking for herbs. You know how stupid you are, don't you?" He gave her a look laden with disappointment.

"I'm sorry, I didn't mean to worry you," Robyn hurried to say. "I was just looking for some herbs I couldn't get at the market but needed for tonight's dinner."

Hunter brushed a loose strand of hair out of her face. "You could have got lost and then what would have happened to me? I would have lost my betrothed and had to live with the knowledge that I failed to save you." Though his words were meant to be tender he still frowned down at her.

"But you would always save me." Robyn tried to erase the stern expression on his face. He must not be mad at her. She hung her head. "I only wanted to cook you a wonderful dinner to prove you had made the right decision in choosing me for a wife."

"But I always make the right decision," he said, his voice a tiny bit cooler than the warmth she was used to. "I do not need a woman who—" His head whipped around. His hands dropped away from her shoulders to hover over the bow draped over his shoulder.

Robyn had heard and seen nothing. "What's wrong?"

"Be quiet, woman!" He hissed.

For several seconds they stood listening to the wind. Robyn could hear nothing else. "Hunter..." she whispered uncertainly. He held his hand up for silence. Her eyes followed his fingers moving to the top of his bootleg for his knife. "Hunter..."

"I told you to—" he began, and then the world turned into a blur and she felt him ripped away from her side.

Robyn fell to the ground, a scream locked in her throat. The pungent smell of the forest filled her senses. Then she heard a growl. It came from directly above her prone body. She tilted her head slightly and stared into the hard blue eyes of a huge white wolf. The scream in her died as fear froze her in place. They stared at each other for a moment, then the wolf growled again, baring its teeth and pawing the ground in front of her. Carefully, she drew her feet back. The wolf eyed her closely, and she immediately stilled, knowing that there was nowhere to run. Robyn had always been told there was nothing inside a wolf but hatred and pleasure in killing, but now she wondered if maybe there was something else, a sentient spark in those glittering blue eyes.

Hunter groaned in pain, breaking the spell. The wolf jumped towards his prone form and bared its fangs. It hunched, ready to attack, huge claws dug into the earth, every fiber in its body shook with pent-up rage. Except it did not leap. Instead, it regarded Hunter as if waiting for him to open his eyes. When he didn't, it roared. Hunter screwed up his eyes tighter and did not move. Robyn realized he was as immobile with fear as she was.

She was taught that a woman must stand by her man, must sacrifice herself to save him. She scrambled unsteadily to her feet and made a lunge. "No!"

Robyn slipped on the wet ground and landed bodily on top of Hunter. She covered him with her smaller body, trying to protect as much of him as possible.

"Please," she said. "Please don't hurt him." Her head was buried in his chest and Robyn could feel the warm breath of the beast on the nape of her neck. It was smelling her. She lay still. If it had to feed, it would feed on her first.

Nothing happened. It stood over them, unmoving. Beneath her, Hunter breathed in fast, shallow gasps. She could feel him tremble. Still nothing happened. Slowly, Robyn turned to look behind her.

The wolf sat a few meters away, its head slightly tilted to one side. It looked as if it was deep in thought. Then it stood and came toward them.

"Please don't kill us," she whispered.

It did not stop, but did not bare its fangs either. Instead, it nuzzled its surprisingly warm nose against her leg where her skirts had rode up. Robyn held her breath and willed herself not to close her eyes. The wolf looked up at her and then gently nipped her calf. She did not feel any pain, though she could see the tiny droplets of blood pooling on her skin. It licked the small wound and stepped back giving her a long, hard look. It seemed to nod at her, as if in some agreement. Then it turned, and jumping delicately disappeared into the thicket.

Robyn realized she was holding her breath. She gave a deep sigh of relief. Beneath her, Hunter stirred and opened his eyes. She knelt beside him watching as he blinked up at her. He tried to sit, and she went to help him but he pushed her hand away. Unaided, he struggled to his feet, grabbing at a branch to steady himself. He was limping.

"Where is it?" he asked in a voice pitched higher than usual.

"It's gone."

"I need my bow. I need to hunt it down."

"It's gone," she repeated. "And you can't follow it in this state."

He glared at her. "This is your fault." He gestured at his ankle.

Robyn was startled at his accusation. Had he forgotten how she'd flung herself across his chest to protect him? She was about to say so when he cut her short.

"If you had done your duty and ordered everything you needed from the market beforehand, you wouldn't have needed to come into the woods. In fact, if you were half as good a woman as I'd imagined, you would have come up with another idea for tonight's dinner." He took a deep breath, sweat building on his brow. "You're reckless and stupid, and you risked my life in trying to save you."

Robyn was downcast, she felt ashamed and a little bit angry. Had she been disobedient? She did not need to ask his permission to come into the woods. At least, not yet. Nor had she asked him to come in after her. He had followed of his own accord, and he had not saved her. He had fainted!

Robyn gasped and slapped a trembling hand over her mouth. Such silly thoughts were not justified. Hunter Wolfmounter was the Beast Slayer, he was her betrothed, and he had come to save her from danger. Who was she to think ill of him? He had every reason to be angry with her.

"Well then." Hunter sighed, his lecture over. He reached out a hand for her. "Be a good girl and let me lean on you." He put his heavy arm around her shoulders. "Let's get out of here." They began to limp back to the village. She tried her best to be strong for him, trying to ignore the throbbing ache beginning in her own leg where the wolf had bitten her.

Just before they reached the market square, Hunter let go of her and straightened to his full height. The Red Riders were gathered by the well waiting to start their night shift. He smoothed his cape before he marched over to them with all the dignity and grace that was expected of the leader of the Red Riders. He walked with the pride of a local hero. His limp no longer holding him back. Robyn followed a few paces behind.

"Another beast hides in the forest," he announced and all heads turned to him. "I have barely saved my betrothed from its claws."

There was uproar as several of his men all talked at once. "My God, Captain! You're wounded!" Hans Sweets, his second in command ran to help him.

Hunter slapped his hurt leg. "Barely a scratch, but enough to stop me from following it." He turned to look at Robyn. "Anyway, I couldn't leave Robyn all alone in the woods to go after the beast." He was brave and proud now he was among his men.

"Why, you as good as saved her life, my friend." Hans was full of praise, as always. "Do you need to see to your wounds?"

Hunter hesitated and looked back at Robyn, who stood several feet away.

"We need to organize a hunt, but first I have to see my betrothed safely home. She'll need escorting to her grandmother's house." He thought for a moment, a dark frown on his handsome face. "Hans, accompany me so we can talk about the hunt." He quickly arranged the village night patrol before he signaled to Hans and Robyn he was ready to leave.

Robyn walked between the men as they turned toward her home. Over her head they planned the hunt.

"It was a big bastard but I managed to scare it away," Hunter said. "It ran deeper into the woods. We'll not go after it tonight."

"We won't?" Hans sounded surprised.

"No. We'll wait until morning, and comb the near side of the forest to make sure it's not lingering close to the village. When we're certain that there is no imminent threat to our people, we'll track it down and kill it!" Hunter's voice was strong and fearless, and rang clearly in Robyn's ears.

It was so cold the tips of her fingers became blue and her lips numb. The only heat was a slow burn in her calf muscle, where the wolf had bit her. She felt nauseous, and searched for Hunters hand under his cloak. He pulled free of her. With blurring vision she forced herself to move forward, not wanting to embarrass him yet again, but her legs soon gave out. The pulsing in her calf mingled with the hammering in her head, finally the last of the strength that kept her upright dissolved. A sickening darkness enveloped her, the only ragged points of light were the broken blue of the white wolf's eyes, concentrating on her, cold and unblinking as she swirled into oblivion.

Waking up was like walking through fire. Every inch of her body burned. Her skin felt so hot she thought it might split open.

"What happened?" She tried to speak, but her words felt dry and heavy on her tongue. Her lips were painfully swollen.

"It's all right, you're home safe and sound." She knew the voice but couldn't place it. With great effort she opened her eyes. Rose was sitting at her bedside. She placed a cold cloth on Robyn's forehead. "Shush, you're fine."

"Where's Hunter?"

Rose rolled her eyes. "He was gone when I arrived. Some boy from the Riders said you'd been attacked by a wolf. Is it true? I'm so sorry, I shouldn't have told you about the damn sage."

"It's not your fault. Hunter was right, I should have thought of something else for dinner. It was stupid of me."

"It was not!" Rose wrung the cloth over the bowl a little too forcefully, and water splashed everywhere. "You're not dead, are you? Whitney told him where to find you. The great Wolfmounter should have been able to save you as well as his own sorry ass."

"Rose," she said weakly. "As you've already pointed out, I'm not dead."

"Are you telling me he saved you?" Rose asked, her voice slick with suspicion.

Robyn was silent. Had Hunter saved her? The wolf could have easily ripped them both apart, but it had not done. It had—well, what exactly had it done? It had spared both their lives and had not wanted anything in return. Or maybe it had?

Rose rearranged her bedclothes and a cry of pain shook Robyn's body. She ached all over from the fever.

"Lie still, I'll try to cool you down." Rose placed wet cloths over her trembling limbs. Every part of her hurt. Except her calf. That was the only place where she didn't feel any pain.

Rose helped her drink some water.

"Where's grandmother?" Robyn asked.

"Downstairs, trying to save the dinner."

Robyn tried to sit up. "The dinner is still taking place? Though Hunter has been hurt?"

"Yes," Rose confirmed, her jaw tight. "The dinner is still taking place even though *you* have been hurt. Hunter will not be dining tonight. He's meeting with the village council to discuss the murderous wolf in the woods."

"But it didn't kill us. It didn't want to." The words were out before she could stop them.

Rose fixed her with an eager stare. Robyn tried her best to meet her gaze, keeping her eyes wide and innocent though the storm of doubt inside her would not ease up.

"What did it do?" Rose crouched beside the bed and placed her hand on Robyn. "What did the wolf do to you?"

Robyn stuttered, "N...nothing."

"Nothing?" Rose was cynical.

Robyn tried to not look away from the accusing stare. "I'm...I'm not sure."

There were many things she was not sure of lately, but she was sure of Rose. She instinctively knew she could trust Rose, the only woman who had an opinion on everything and openly expressed it. Rose was brave, but she could also be foolhardy. She had not always been like that. Robyn remembered when, as little girls, the twins had barely differed. But at some point on becoming young women,

Rose had become difficult while Whitney had remained the lovely, submissive girl everybody expected her to be.

"I think the wolf bit me," Robyn stated quietly.

Rose pressed her lips together but said nothing.

"Hunter was unconscious and I flung myself over him to stop it from killing him." Rose snorted. Robyn ignored her and continued, "It did stop, but it bit me instead. On the back of my leg. Then it went away." It was still a mystery to her. Why hadn't the wolf killed them both?

Rose sighed and looked away. "You must not tell anyone," she said, turning her worried gaze back to Robyn. "I'll say you're exhausted and in shock, and you need to rest for a while. So, no visitors, okay?" Rose's grip on her hand became painful. "You'll tell nobody about the bite. Do you understand?"

"Why? What's wrong?" Robyn asked, fearfully.

Rose saw her fear and softened. She loosened her grip on Robyn's hand and softly stroked her cheek. "Nothing. But you can't tell anyone that Hunter Wolfmounter, the great Beast Slayer, swooned away when the wolf came calling." She spat out the words.

"He didn't swoon. He passed out." Robyn still felt compelled to protect him.

"Sure. Whatever you want to believe."

Through her fog of pain Robyn could not grasp what was really behind Rose's words, though she knew some strong emotion lingered there. With a shake of her head, Rose once again became the jolly caregiver. She arose from her seat and moved to the door. "I'll get you some broth," she said, as if nothing had happened. "You need to rest now."

Robyn awoke sweating and unsettled several hours later. Cold, blue eyes had haunted her fitful sleep. If she squeezed her eyes shut the image of a huge wolf outside her window appeared in her mind. She moved her head; it was not hurting anymore. The fever had broken. Rose was asleep in a chair beside her bed. Robyn wriggled her hand under her covers and tried to reach the bite on the back of her leg. Her fingers traced six raised bumps where her skin had been penetrated. They were surprisingly small given the size of the beast's teeth.

She lay back and closed her eyes, but sleep didn't come. Instead, she remembered the events in the forest. Hunter had certainly not saved her, he had pretended to be unconscious while she cried out for help. Appalled by the sudden thought, she looked over to Rose, certain the other woman would be shaken awake by the sheer wickedness of her thoughts. Rose was fast asleep and Robyn breathed a sigh of relief. Hunter was a brave, upright man and she mustn't think otherwise of him. Still, Robyn couldn't see the necessity to kill the wolf just because it had defended its territory.

Of course, it had been different seven years ago when the Black Wolf had devastated their village, frightening the men and attacking the women. Hunter had been a hero then, chasing the terrifying creature into the woods and cutting its head off. The huge wolf head still hung from the rafters in Spindlefinger's inn. It reminded them all why Hunter Wolfmounter lead the Red Riders. And now he was to repeat his valiant action in search of another trophy. But what if Robyn's senses hadn't betrayed her and Hunter had pretended to be unconscious rather than fight? Of course, as a woman she was not allowed to think of her betrothed as a liar. He must have had his reasons and she was just too dull to understand. Maybe Rose would help her figure that out in the morning. Although, there was no love lost between Rose and Hunter and whatever Robyn told her that might discredit Hunter, Rose would no doubt eventually use against him. What would that make Robyn? Certainly not a good wife.

Chapter 3

Robyn sat near the window and used the remaining sunlight to mend the tear in her skirt. It had been a week since the attack and she felt remarkably better. The fever had gone, and Rose came by every day to bring her herbs for the wound on her leg. She did not stay to help her dress it; there was nothing to clean. The bite had healed completely leaving six little hard lumps that were only visible if you knew where to look.

"Be a good girl and chop these for me." Granny placed a knife and onions on the table in front of her.

"What are you cooking?" Robyn started stripping off the onion skins.

"Peter, the new Rider in training, is coming by to collect some stew for Captain Wolfmounter and his men. It's a cold day, and they are doing dangerous work. It's the most we can do to provide them with warm bellies when they come back from the hunt."

"We could go and search with them." The words were out before she could stop them.

Granny pointed her wooden spoon at her accusingly. "And do a man's work! Did you hit your head out there, girl?" She crossed her arms, grim-faced. "If you hadn't been so reckless and gone to the woods in the first place the Riders would not need to go in search of that monster!" Her grandmother rarely spoke to her loudly. And she hadn't lectured Robyn as yet about straying into the woods, mostly because she was still unwell. It seemed her rest was over.

"I'm sorry for scaring you."

"You did not scare me, you disappointed my trust in you, and you put the Captain in danger." Granny clarified her position.

"But isn't Hunter supposed to save me?" The snide remark embarrassed even her.

For a moment, her grandmother stared at her openmouthed. "My dear girl, I can only assume your wits have been frightened out of you, for I will not allow you to speak like that about your future husband! What would you do without him? He asked for your hand, even though you are a poor match with no parents and no dowry. Captain Hunter Wolfmounter is a great man, and he will be able to train you in all those things I could not. You should be grateful to have the chance to marry above your station, but instead you speak ill of your betrothed!"

"Granny, I…I…" Robyn stammered. She didn't understand where her evil thoughts had come from. Why was she speaking in such a disrespectful way about Hunter? "I didn't mean to question his bravery. It's just the wolf didn't do anything, it just…"

"Didn't do anything? It didn't do anything? It threatened your life, silly girl! If Hunter hadn't had the presence of mind to follow you into the woods, why, you could be dead now. What would people think of me as your guardian if that happened? You didn't listen to my orders, and now poor Hunter is the one to pay."

Robyn laid the knife down and tried to reason with her. "All I wanted was to say that—"

"No!" her grandmother said. "You will say nothing more. Those brave men are out there taking care of us. We should be grateful that they are willing to do so. We couldn't survive without their help."

"Do you really think we are useless without men?"

Her grandmother did not dignify her with an answer; she turned away and stirred the stewpot. Her silence did not last long.

"Go upstairs and gather the laundry. And if you dare to speak like that again, I will never forgive you. How could you shame me in front of your future husband? Letting him see how I failed him in providing a good girl for his wife." Granny was near to tears. Robyn could not respond. "Go now, and do as you're told for once."

Robyn went upstairs. The onions rolled across the table untouched.

"The snows will come before we find it," Hans said, exasperated.

Hunter slammed his tankard down on the table. "I know, but it has to be near, we have to find it."

Here in the Red Rider's headquarters they were pouring over a map of the forest and the surrounding villages. All possible hiding places for the beast were marked out.

Candles illuminated the men's stern faces. It had been a long fruitless search.

A soft knock came to the door. The man nearest answered. "It's your sister, sir," he told Hans.

"She's brought food for the hunt." Hans signaled to let her in.

Greta carefully entered the room. She was some years younger than Hans but already her rare beauty was spoken of far and wide. As her brother was the right-hand man of the captain of the Red Riders, her prospects of a good marriage were high. Some of the Riders had already approached Hans to ask for her hand and discuss a marriage settlement. Hunter knew he hadn't decided on anyone yet. Greta was still young and there was no hurry. He supposed it was a disappointment to Hans that she had not caught Hunter's own eye, but what Hans didn't know was that he found the girl too insolent. He disliked the direct way she looked him in the eye. It was not suitable behavior for a girl. She was far too sure of herself and what she wanted for Hunter's taste.

While Greta handed over her food packages, Hunter turned back to the map and its markers.

"We can't reach half of these places if the weather turns against us," he said. "Especially if snow covers up the wolf's tracks. If we catch it at all, it has to be now before the snows fall."

"Why don't you wait until spring?" Greta's light, feminine voice filled the room. "I mean, what if the beast has already settled in for the winter? It might not even be in the area anymore. It might be in the caves up in the hills."

Silence fell, and all eyes turned to Greta. Hunter gave Hans a hard look. Immediately, Hans took Greta by her arm and escorted her to the door. The grip wasn't as forceful as Hunter would have liked, and though his words were muted, they at least seemed to have the desired effect. Greta shrank back and nodded before hurriedly leaving.

"I'm sorry..." Hans began.

"No need." Hunter held his hand up. "It happened once and never will again. She is young. You still have time for discipline." He pointed at the map, bringing the focus back to the business at hand. "All right, we'll go north tonight," Hunter ordered, and started dividing his men into hunting parties.

Robyn listened to the wind rattling around the house. A night bird sang a sad little song in the tree outside her window. She sat in the middle of the floor amid piles of dirty laundry. Compelled to see the bird, Robyn moved onto her knees to take a look. It sat on a lower branch, its tiny chest swollen as it proudly sang.

It occurred to her that it was strange she could see it so well in the muted evening light. Her vision had become sharper. There was also a strange odor that—the singing died...along with the bird. All that was left was a single downy feather dangling from the white wolf's jaws. Robyn gasped.

The wolf cast a glance at her window as if it knew she was there. Then it turned away, and its huge, ghostly body vanished into the darkness. Robyn stared after it, her nose pressed against the glass, her fingernails digging into the wood of the windowsill. If anybody saw it now, right here in the village, the Riders would kill it.

Before she thought anymore about it, she grabbed her cape and opened the window. The gnarled tree limbs were within easy reach, and, feeling strangely unafraid she climbed out onto the nearest branch. Within minutes she had scrambled to the ground and was running after the wolf, uncaring that it could kill her as easily as it had the poor bird. Instead, she ran faster and prayed she would catch up with it before the Riders did.

The men were gathered outside, some tending to the horses, some inspecting their weapons for the last time. Hunter was leaving the Red Rider's headquarters when Peter came running up.

"What is it?" he asked, as the lad skidded to a halt before him.

"Your betrothed, sir," he said. "Granny has just discovered that she's sneaked out the upstairs window."

Hunter's spine stiffened. He hadn't seen Robyn since the incident at the woods. She should have come by to check on his wound and make sure he was okay, but instead she had stayed home pleading a fever as an excuse to neglect him. He had vowed to be patient and kind, at least until they were married. He wanted to be a fine husband who took the time to accustom his wife to her new home and duties. He had waited for her, and how had she thanked him? By discrediting him in front of his men and running away again.

"Thank you, Peter." He patted the boy's shoulder "Find Hans for me and then go and join your unit."

Hunter began to frantically think of where Robyn might have gone. Who were her friends in the village? Who would know?

"Sir?" Hans appeared at his side.

Hunter put an arm awkwardly around his shoulder, for he was at least one head smaller than Hunter, and led him away from the men. The fainted scent of chocolate reached his nostrils. "I have a minor problem and my hands are full at the moment."

"Of course, sir, what will you have me do?"

"It's a private matter."

Hans looked up at him with furrowed brows. "What is it, Hunter?"

"Apparently Robyn has sneaked out of the house. Her grandmother has just sent word to me."

Hans blinked stupidly for a moment; then a knowing smile spread across his face. "I think she might be looking for your attention, Captain. After all, you've been very busy with the wolf hunt."

"Why can't she be a good girl and wait at home until I find the time to call," Hunter said, with a sigh. "But no. She waits until now to deliberately make me angry. I need to concentrate on the beast, but she plays hide and seek with me."

Hans said, "Don't let this little lover's game distract you. Every girl runs away sooner or later, and then it's her betrothed's task to chase her."

"I thought she would be sensible enough to not require so much wooing. She grew up without a father, she should be thankful I am willing to take care of her." Anger showed through his words.

"Captain, a little struggle is to be expected. You just said that Robyn has never experienced the strong hand of a father. You will have to be both husband and father to her. She needs taming, and the Wolfmounter is just the man to do it. You need to show her how it will be once she's your wife."

"You're a great man, Hans," Hunter said. "As the only protector of your sister you have become wise beyond your years when it comes to women."

Hans nodded in agreement. "I will look for her discreetly while you track down the beast."

Hunter looked at his Second-in-Command, his chest filling with pride and relief at having such a good and pliable friend by his side.

The fever may have weakened her body but Robyn wasn't too out of breath. The forest lay dark and foreboding before her and the wolf had disappeared into that darkness. If she wanted to find it, she had to follow. She needed to find it. The Riders would track and kill the poor creature if Robyn couldn't warn it off. Taking a deep breath to calm her racing heart, she lifted her skirts and stepped forward. Why couldn't women wear trousers? It would be much more useful. She bit her lip. Where had that thought come from? She liked her long skirts, she had never thought about wearing men's clothing before, so why now?

The faraway hoot of an owl shook her out of her thoughts. Carefully, she moved deeper into the forest. The earth was soft under her feet, though her steps sounded loud to her own ears. Above her, the trees slowly swayed in the wind. Under the branches it was warmer than out in the open. The huge trees shut out the cold but left oppressive darkness. Small animals leaped from branch to branch overhead, their rustling raised the hairs on her neck.

A twig snapped nearby. She froze. Her breathing slowed as she strained to listen. No other noise came.

"Are you here?" she whispered. "I swear I will not harm you." Nothing but silence. The entire forest had grown still. "Please, you do not have to show yourself, just listen. The men are on their way here. They will kill you if you don't leave."

There was nothing there, but she could smell a new odor, and knew the wolf wasn't far away. With a sigh she grabbed at her skirt, readying to head back home again.

"If you hear me," she left one last piece of advice. "Please go north as far as you can. The snows will come soon and they will not be able to track you."

Was she mad standing in the forest talking to a phantom on a freezing night? Advising a fearsome beast to run before her betrothed slayed it? She started to walk away when something warm and furry brushed against her hand. She jumped.

The wolf sat in front of her watching her intently, its head cocked slightly. Its piercing blue eyes looked her up and down and she had the feeling it would pounce at any unexpected move.

"Can you understand what I'm saying?" she asked, her heart hammering. It bent its head and kept staring.

"So you heard me?" Again a soft nod. "They are coming to kill you."

The wolf stood up and moved towards her, very slowly, its head down. Strangely, she did not feel any fear. She stood still and let it come close. It put its massive head under her cold hand and waited. Robyn held her breath. What was she doing? If Hunter was ever to find out he would break the engagement instantly and make her unwelcome to the whole village. She had not only disobeyed village law, but the orders of her grandmother and her betrothed. Why was she doing this? Was it the fever from the bite? Was that why she had started thinking, started questioning herself and everything she knew?

The beast didn't look so monstrous, not now she was stroking its head. Still, it was a huge wolf. Its shoulders reached as high as her ribs, and its head could easily rest on her shoulder. She stroked down the soft neck, the fur running like silk between her fingers. It was so white and clean it could glow in the moonlight if only there were some. It was dark in the woods but still she could see the wolf's fur as if it were in daylight. Her hand stilled, and the wolf looked up at her.

"Should I be afraid of you?" she asked.

Chapter 4

While his men patrolled the village, Hunter waited on the western road for Hans. Soon he appeared stumbling along the stony path, his way illuminated by his oil lamp. He shook his head as he approached.

"No sign of her on the streets. She may be hiding at a friend's house, but I didn't want to go knocking on people's doors looking for a disobedient girl at this time of night. I ordered young Peter to stay put outside her house, in case she comes back."

Hunter kicked at a pebble. "Peter is a loyal lad, he will become a good Rider someday. As for Robyn, you were right not to wake anyone, but do I really have to wait until morning to find her in some friend's house? What does she expect to happen?"

"Look, it has probably something to do with her menstruation. They always get emotional then. Women can't think rationally at the best of times. Believe me, if you tell her exactly how to behave she will be grateful for it, and willing to obey you."

Hunter willed himself to relax. "I underestimated this. I thought I knew her and would be able to train her. I see I was naive."

"Ho there! Who is it?" came a guard's shout.

Hans and Hunter followed the call and found a woman, huddled in a thick cloak, standing in a pool of lamplight. Two Riders stood over her. For a second Hunter thought it was Robyn.

"Rose Prospector?" Hans recognized the girl. "What is she doing here?"

"What do you want, girl?" Hunter was angry that he had got his hopes up and guessed wrong.

Rose came over to stand before him. "I was running errands and bumped into your little patrol."

Hunter narrowed his eyes. Aside from her impertinent tone she irritated him by not dropping her gaze when she spoke to him. Instead, she stood looking directly at him.

"You're running errands in the middle of the night. What errands?" Hans asked, always the pragmatist. Rose did not break her gaze from Hunter; nor did she answer Hans.

"Why are you staring at me, woman?" Hunter snapped.

She snorted and looked him up and down with obvious distaste. "You're a fake, Wolfmounter, and I know it. Nobody here will ever believe me, but I can still say it to your face."

Hans had stepped forward and grabbed her arm. "Mind your manners." She did not flinch.

Hans looked to Hunter for further instructions. It would have been easy to let Hans throw her in the cells for a night, but his guts told him not to risk it.

"Do you know Robyn's whereabouts?" he asked, and thought he saw something flicker in her eyes. "Her grandmother reported her missing. You were nursing her after the attack; did she seem upset? Did she say anything to you?"

"Oh, she did," Rose smiled, making him uncomfortable. "But nothing about running away from you."

"I warned you to guard your tongue," Hans spoke softly. His grip tightened. Still, Rose did not react at all and kept her gaze locked with Hunter's.

"I don't know where Robyn is, but I am glad that someone has finally bitten some sense into her." She spoke slowly and clearly and made sure he heard every word.

His vision blurred. Had Robyn noticed him faking unconsciousness? His mind raced. What if she hadn't run away to get his attention after all, but rather to tell people of his cowardice? He was fairly sure that she had seen no one this past week, except for the Prospector girl, and who would believe that little witch when it was his word against hers? Nevertheless, he couldn't be sure. He had to find Robyn and silence her!

"Captain!" Peter came running. The boy came to a halt gulping for air. "It's Robyn, sir," he managed to say. "I was on my way over to her grandmother's cottage when I saw her going into the woods. I tried to catch up with her but she was too far ahead. She didn't hear me calling her. I thought it best to come and tell you instead of going after her alone."

Hunter tried his best to hold himself together. He glanced over at Hans who pushed an appalled Rose away and came over to him.

"What will you have us do, sir?" Peter asked.

"Be quiet, boy." Hans put a hand on Hunter's shoulder. "She is not lost yet, my friend. We will go with you into the woods, and if the beast goes after her, you can slay it, just like you did before."

Hunter felt the blood drain from his face. He thought frantically for a way to avoid going to the woods. If only the stupid girl would get eaten by the wolf all his problems would be solved. But he was Hunter Wolfmounter, slayer of beasts, he could not be seen evading this task or he would lose everything.

"She is my betrothed," he said and placed his hand on his heart. "I will not risk any of my men to get her back. I will go alone."

"And that is the reason we will follow you, Captain," Hans said, slightly bewildered.

"There is no need for that," Hunter tried again. "I will find her and bring her back safely."

"Sir, we know you're the bravest and most honorable man in the whole kingdom, but there is no need for you to fight alone."

"I'm responsible for your safety and I cannot risk losing even one of you to this reckless situation."

"It is not reckless, we've been searching for the beast the whole week. In fact, all the more reason to catch it while we can."

Hunter closed his eyes in frustration. Yes, he was such a good leader that his men would die for him. There was no other way out. They would enter the woods as one unit.

"All right." He gave in. "To arms, men. Follow me. We have a beast to slay."

The wolf sat motionless at Robyn's side while she stroked its head. Its presence somehow calmed her and made her focus on the odd events of the past few days.

Her grandmother had never yelled at her before. And Robyn had never raised her voice back, especially not over such nonsense as independent thinking. Soon she would become Hunter's wife. Once, she had believed that would fill her with pride, but not anymore, and she now doubted if it ever had.

Granny was proud she had captured the Red Rider's eye. While some girls were jealous of her, many of the men were openly doubtful that she was equal to the task. Robyn had never felt any joy at being his betrothed. Part of her was happy to finally be like all the other women in the village, to have a husband to take care of, and a household to organize, and maybe even children to nurse one day. She would no longer be the pitied orphan girl but a respected part of female society. So why was she standing here, in the middle of the night, with Hunter's sworn enemy and feeling relieved that she had come all this way into the woods to warn it?

The wolf cocked its ears, then rose to its feet. Robyn strained to hear whatever it had heard, but there was nothing but silence. The wolf watched her intently, those blue eyes burning into her. She concentrated again. And then...yes, there they were. Footsteps. Many of them.

"You need to run and hide," she whispered. The wolf nudged her hip. Its cold nose brushed her fingers. It bumped gently against her again, trying to move her in the direction she had come from.

Robyn realized that it wanted her to flee. Why did it care that she must not be seen here? The wolf growled softly and Robyn said, "You have to go." She made shooing gestures with her hands. The wolf turned away and slid into the undergrowth and was out of sight in two massive strides.

Now she just had to find her own way back home.

Hunter crouched behind the bushes, frantically thinking of a way to get away from the search party and find the girl before they did.

A rustle came from the undergrowth. It couldn't be the beast, he was sure it wasn't that stupid. But nevertheless he could use the distraction to get the space he wanted. He turned to the men crouched close behind him.

"I'll go this way," he ordered quietly. "Hans, take the men and come in from the other side."

Hans looked unsure. "What if—"

"That's an order. I won't take a chance. Go!"

Hans gathered the men and slid away in the opposite direction. Finally alone, Hunter waited until the Riders were far enough away before moving closer to the noise, hoping desperately he'd got it right and this wasn't a huge wolf, after all. It would be terribly inconvenient to die now and let that girl run around desecrating his memory by exposing all his lies and failings.

He slunk behind a tree, his shaking hands aiming his bow and arrow at everything that moved. A twig cracked. He peeked around the tree trunk and caught a flash of red hair running through the trees. Without thinking twice, he aimed and let loose his arrow. *What? Wasn't it the wolf? I've killed my lovely? Oh, dear, how frustrating.*

He looked again. No sign of her. Hopefully, that meant the girl was down. He moved out from his cover, notched another arrow, and stepped carefully toward where he had last seen her. There she was, and she was still standing. His shot missed. She looked toward him with huge, helpless eyes, an easy target. Too easy. He couldn't shoot from this distance. It would be obvious he had made no mistake this close. She made no move to run. She probably thought she could stand there until the rest of the Riders appeared, so she could tell them about that fateful night in the woods, and his fear of the wolf.

He drew his bow, aiming directly at her heart. She had to die. He would think up some lie afterwards. Maybe brigands had killed her? His men would believe anything he told them.

"Captain!"

Damn them all! Who the hell shouted out in a forest full of wild beasts and murderous thugs? There was no time now. They were too close.

"Run," he told her. "Run and never look back! If you ever set foot in the village again, I will kill you."

Still she didn't move.

His arrow thudded into the earth next to her feet. "Run!" Finally, she did.

He wiped his brow with shaking fingers, hoping she would heed his advice and stay away. It wasn't the best solution, but the most practical at hand. Now he had to make it look like she would never be seen again.

He was gathering his arrows back into his quiver when he saw her shoe lying in the dirt. She'd lost it in her scramble to get away from him. He smiled. A shoe paired with his stagecraft, would do the trick nicely.

He pulled his hunting knife from his boot, pushed aside his trouser leg and slid the blade gently across the skin. A thin line of blood appeared. He smeared it over the shoe.

Someone was crashing through the undergrowth toward him. He adjusted his pant leg as Hans burst through the trees, his men not far behind him.

"Captain!" He was panting hard. "We lost the wolf, sir!"

"I know," he said in a quivering voice. "It came back here and took Robyn away, right before my eyes. I was too late. She was already lifeless. The beast was too fast and I couldn't get a good shot at it. Now all I have left is this." He produced the bloodied shoe and showed it as the final proof.

His men stood with bowed heads, unsure what to say. "I'm so sorry, Hunter." Hans was the first to speak. "I take it we can't go after it?"

"I doubt it. I got one chance, and I failed. This, this is my punishment." He indicated the shoe again. His shoulders slumped, and he let despair flood his face.

"We will come back in first daylight, and if we cannot find it, we will return in the spring and kill it." Hans tried to console him. "I promise you will be avenged, my friend."

"I will slay it!" Hunter said, his voice proud and full of vengeance. "I'll cut out its heart, and hang its filthy head next to that other damned creature." Inside he hoped he would never have to face either the beast or that stupid girl again.

Robyn had no idea how far she had run into the forest. The air was thick and moist, and the light had an eerie green tinge. She stumbled onward, her bare foot cut and bloody, until she was sure another arrow was not going to skim past her shoulder. Slowing down, she finally took a moment to breathe. Hunter had tried to kill her! Maybe that first shot had been a mistake, but then he had stepped out of nowhere and aimed again, at her heart! And she could do nothing to save herself but stand there frozen with shock. She looked down at her trembling hands.

If Hans hadn't shouted, she would be dead now. She had no doubt about that. Hunter had meant to kill her, and Hans had inadvertently saved her.

She looked around. The light among the trees was so dim that it was hard to tell if it was dawn or dusk.

Robyn huddled into her cape. Her shaking increased now she had stopped running. Hunter had tried to kill her. The man she should have married wanted her dead. It felt so unreal. But she knew she couldn't go back home, he would be waiting for her. And nobody would protect her from the captain of the Red Riders.

She was alone now. There was no one to rescue her. No knight in shining armor was going to jump out of the bushes to save her. She looked over her shoulder still afraid Hunter was following her, about to loom out of the shadows ready to kill. Except it wasn't that dark. She could see very well, given how far into the woods she had run. In fact, up ahead she could make out a small clearing. Should she go there? The moment she stepped out of the trees she would be an open target.

The rustling of leaves behind her made her blood freeze. Had Hunter followed her after all? She turned around slowly, expecting to see him with his bow raised. Her scream died in her throat. There was no Hunter. Only the white wolf. It sprang at her, bringing her to the ground. It bared its fangs and growled inches from her face. The forest swirled above her head and what little light there was grew dimmer. Her last conscious thought was the surprise in the wolf's icy blue eyes before the darkness swallowed her.

They drank a toast to him. All the Red Riders met up at Spindlefinger's inn to pay their respects and drink with their captain. Glasses were raised in respect for his loss. Robyn was a pretty young thing. Such a waste. And they also drank in commiseration for the missed chance of slaying the wolf that had killed her. Hunter knew that privately a lot of the men thought she had turned out to be a handful, and this was the fate that befell willful, silly girls. Spindlefinger had put up drinks on the house, so there were many sad toasts and proud boasts of vengeance on all the evil creatures that lived in the forest.

Hunter had already been to Granny's house to inform her of her granddaughter's demise. Her reaction had been tearful, but she had been glad that the beast hadn't caught him. What would the villagers do without their captain, she had told him, especially with bloodthirsty wolves lurking in the woods?

The massive black wolf's head hung above his chair as a trophy of his bravery. In his drunken haze it seemed to sway in the torchlight, nodding in defiance at him. The hollow, dead eyes stared down in accusation. It angered him. He had killed this ugly creature and launched his career as a hero, and here it was mocking him, *him,* the famous Wolfmounter!

"Damn it!" He slammed his tankard on the table, splashing Hans with beer.

"Captain," Hans said, totally misunderstanding as usual. "It's not your fault. She shouldn't have been there. If you couldn't save her then no one could."

There was a moment of silence between them.

"And so close to the wedding," Spindlefinger muttered sadly, bringing another tankard to the table to replace the spilled one.

Hunter's head jerked upwards. The wedding arrangements! The orders from the bakery! The bridal linens! Nevermind the fact that he had already paid Spindlefinger for the wedding feast. All that wine, and food, and ale, for a wedding that would never be. He was out a fortune! Maybe he could get Hans to cancel it for him and make sure he got his money back? One look at Spindlefinger's sly face told him he'd be lucky. Hunter slumped into a real bad mood as opposed to the fake one he was providing for his men.

The inn door swung open and the cold bite of air brought Rose Prospector in along with it. Hunter scowled. He had forgotten all about her. She sailed across the floor straight for him, ignoring the calls of the other patrons that this was no place for a young woman and she should leave. His heart began to hammer in his chest and he tried to calm himself.

Hans rose to his feet, and Hunter assumed he was about to escort the ignorant girl back outside when he noticed Hans was not paying attention to Rose. His eyes were on his sister, Greta, who had followed Rose into the tavern.

"Miss Prospector," Hunter said, in the most authoritative tone he could muster. "Are you still roaming the streets?" His eyes narrowed with warning, but she came on until she was standing before him.

"What happened to Robyn?" she hissed between closed teeth. The look that she gave him was insolent and unforgiving. He had to stop himself from slapping her. She hadn't been there, so she couldn't have seen anything, he reminded himself.

"I tried to save her." He hoped the sad face he had been wearing all night would fool her as much as it had his men. "I feel terrible. I have failed her, failed the village, and failed my vows."

"You failed your vows long ago," she said, softly. So softly he had to lean forward to hear it. He pulled back, trying to hide his anger. He had to get her out of here before she did something rash. From the corner of his eye he could see Hans rebuking his sister.

"You are no threat to me," he answered, equally quietly. "Are you sure you are safe here, in a tavern full of men?"

He was aware all eyes were on them. No one was in earshot, and he assumed it looked like Rose was upset and asking about her friend. She was a risk, though. He did not need her aggressive, uncontrolled attitude, but he could hardly take her out to the forest then blame wolves for her disappearance. No village was that careless with its young women.

"Rose." The low warning call came from Greta. Rose continued to watch him through narrowed eyes, but he could see uncertainty there. She had no idea what had happened in the woods. Robyn had ran away and would never come back. Self-assurance flowed through him. He was safe. He was the captain of the Red Riders and he owned this village, and no little chit of a girl was going to face him down in his own chair, in his own tavern, and under the head of his own damned trophy!

"Rose Prospector, you need to learn your place and it's certainly not among drinking men in a tavern. I thank you for your concern regarding the loss of my betrothed. And now you'll have to leave before I report your night time activities to your father." He snapped his fingers and two of his men approached. "Escort Miss Prospector home. It's dangerous out there. We have a killer on the loose with a taste for female flesh."

She looked straight into his eyes, her whole body shaking with anger. He tried not to smile as she was taken away. Hans took his sister's arm and led her to the door along with the escort, all the while speaking quietly and intently to her. His words worked. Greta left looking suitably dejected. The door closed behind the young women and the volume in the inn cranked up as business returned to normal.

Hans returned to the table looking mortified. Hunter held up his hand. "Don't blame your sister," he said. "It's the Prospector girl and her impossible behavior. Greta came in to try and calm her down. Some chance! I advise you to forbid Greta to meet with that girl. She's a disgrace of a woman."

Hans nodded in agreement. "Yes. Mud sticks. But sometimes Greta gets these weird ideas into her head and it takes forever to get her back into her right mind."

Hunter watched Hans carefully. "She looks good and ripe. Maybe it's time to find her a decent man. She's straining against her brother's will to make you see that she is ready for a husband."

Hans leaned back in his chair and sighed. "You're probably right. I'll think about it tomorrow. There have been offers. Greta is a lovely girl." He barked out a laugh. "I'm luckier than old Darwin, though. Who'd want to marry Rose Prospector? Poor Whitney, she's great wife material but Darwin will never offload her with that harpy for a sister."

Nodding agreement, Hunter drank his ale. The cold fluid run down his throat, and lightning struck his brain. He knew how to shut the stupid Prospector girl up once and for all. And he didn't even need to kill her. He put his tankard down on the table and considered his plan before turning to Hans.

"Old Prospector should face it, nobody will ever want Rose. But the sister is another deal altogether."

Hans nodded. "She was the one who told you Robyn went to the woods. She even knew where to go to find her. That shows a million times more common sense than her sister."

“And no one will take her because of the sister?” Hunter wanted to make sure.

“No. Darwin’s had to go out of the village to fish for a husband for her. Poor bastard.”

“I will marry her!” Hunter declared.

“What!”

“I will marry Britney—”

“Whitney.”

“Whatever.” Hunter took another chug from his tankard.

“Her name is Whitney.” Hans was looking at him funny, probably worried he was too drunk.

“I need a wife, Hans,” Hunter said. Trying to pass off what must seem like a wild mood swing. “I’m ready for a wife. It’s been arranged for many months. My position in the village and with the Red Riders demands I settle down. My bachelor days are over.” He smiled and was glad to see Hans smile back.

“But Rose will be part of your family?” he asked hesitantly.

“All the better for her,” Hunter said confidently. “Her father made a sorry mess raising her. But she deserves better than to sit minding him into his old age. No. She’ll come to my house along with her sister and help raise the children and run the household. And in return I will turn her into an obedient, graceful woman.” *And I can keep an eye on her and her big mouth.*

“Two for the price of one.” Hans laughed and took a long haul from his tankard.

“Yes,” Hunter slapped his back.

“You are a kind and good man,” Hans said, obviously affected by the generosity of his friend. “She will be difficult, you know.”

"I am man enough for the job. And I can always marry her off when she is broken in." Hunter laughed heartily.

"So it is settled then." Hans raised his tankard in a toast.

"Yes. Tomorrow I will go to Prospector's house and ask for the hand of his beloved Sidney."

"Whitney."

"Of course."

Both men clashed tankards in a salute to a brilliant plan.

Chapter 5

A SHARP SLAP ACROSS HER face woke her. She blinked slowly, her eyes sticky and swollen, and found Hunter's angry face looming over her. He pressed his hand against her mouth.

"Shush, lovely," he hissed in her ear. "You don't want the beast to find us, do you?"

But the beast had already found her. She had been tricked into thinking the wolf was her attacker. No. Not the wolf. It was Hunter pressing her down against the cold earth. Hunter staring down at her in triumph. How had it come to this? When had he started to despise her? When had he become the villain instead of the hero of her dreams?

Robyn kicked out hard, trying to break free. She couldn't let him win. She couldn't let him have his way with her. Whatever wrong she had done, she didn't deserve to die for it!

Gathering all her strength, she opened her mouth and bit his once caressing hand as hard as she could. He yelped and pulled away. Too late she saw the knife. It flashed viciously as he plunged it in her chest again and again and—She sat bolt upright and screamed.

Shards of daylight ripped through her dream. Pain burned through her head, and also through her arm. She gasped at the sting of it.

"Be careful. You've injured your arm. I had to bandage it." A strange voice spoke from somewhere nearby.

Robyn tried to focus on her surroundings. She was in a cabin, lying on a comfortable bed under a warm quilt. Far away from Hunter. She noticed her clothes drying near the fireplace. Her clothes? With a start she pulled the blankets higher.

"You hit your head. You need to take it easy, lass," the voice continued.

Robyn was confused. Was Rose scolding her? Except the voice didn't sound like Rose. Then a strange woman came into view, so different from Rose that Robyn almost laughed at her mistake. This woman had flaxen hair, so short it barely covered her ears. And on her legs... *Were those trousers?*

"Who are you?" Robyn asked.

The woman took the bedside chair and sat down.

"How long have I been here?" Robyn asked again. "Where are we? How did you find me? What—"

The woman's laugh cut her short. "So many questions."

"What do you mean?"

"And there you go again." The woman smiled, but it was not very friendly, and Robyn dropped her gaze. The stranger was right, asking questions was not the polite way for a woman to start a conversation, even one who feared she'd been abducted.

While she was scared by not knowing where she was, Robyn realized she was not frightened of the woman.

With her good hand, she touched her bandaged arm. She flinched. The image of the wolf attacking her loomed in her mind. She remembered falling, and then only darkness.

"Did you see it?" She couldn't help but ask again, no matter how rude.

"See what?"

"The wolf."

"Wolf?"

"Yes." Robyn resisted the urge to shake the woman. "The wolf that attacked me. I blacked out and woke up here. Did you see it?"

The woman stood, towering over the bed with arms crossed. "It attacked you?" she asked, her tone clipped.

It hurt Robyn to tilt her head back and look up at her. Instead, she redirected her gaze to the woman's leather boots. She dressed very oddly. "I am not sure," she confessed. "I don't think it wanted to hurt me, I—"

"She, not 'It'," the woman interrupted. "It's a she-wolf."

Robyn did look up now. Pain shot through her head. "How do you know?" she managed to ask. "Is she all right? Did they get her?"

The woman turned away. "Again, so many questions."

"Well, you could try to answer for a change." Silence hung in the air, and Robyn inwardly cringed. If she'd talked back to a man like that she would have been punished. She didn't know what to expect from this strange woman.

Suddenly, the stranger knelt beside the bed and took Robyn's cold hand in her warm one.

"The wolf is fine. Nobody harmed her", she said, her voice becoming gentle. "Those idiots didn't dare go after—"

"You cannot call the Red Riders idiots!" Robyn said, shocked.

The woman laughed and pulled her hands away, leaving Robyn's fingers to grow cold again. "Aye, lass, I can and I will. This is my cabin, and I can say anything I want here. If you want to stay, you should keep that in mind."

"Stay?" Robyn looked up into the hard face. Eyes, no more than narrow slits of bright blue pinned her to the bed. She had the boldest, coldest eyes Robyn had ever seen in a woman. "I can stay here?" Robyn managed to ask.

The woman shrugged her shoulders and gestured to the door. "Or leave if you want."

"No," Robyn said, quickly, then, "Maybe. I mean, I don't even know you, and you haven't met me before. What makes you think you could trust me?"

"At last, a clever question."

Was it? As a woman, she was not supposed to ask questions at all, let alone clever ones.

"Listen, lass, I found you lying in the forest with an injured arm. The wolf didn't harm you; your injuries came from your fall. The wolf is no threat to you," she said. "You were a problem to me, though. If I left you there, you might have died, and I didn't want people snooping around looking for you." Her smile took the edge off her words. "I decided a wee thing like you couldn't be that much trouble."

"Thank you," Robyn said, the woman's smile made her feel a little bolder. "But I don't even know your name. And what are you doing out here in the forest? Do you live here with your husband?"

The woman's face turned to stone. "I live alone. This is my house, my land, my home. I run things around here, and I'll make sure it stays that way."

"Thank you for letting me stay," Robyn whispered, worried she had angered her host.

The woman shrugged. "There was little choice."

Robyn fell silent and stared at her bandaged arm. Her host was wrong to be worried. No hero would come to her rescue. Her hero was the man she was fleeing from. No other help was to be expected. She had betrayed her village by warning the wolf the Riders were coming for it. Or was 'it' a 'her', now she knew it's gender?

Even Granny would disown her. Hunter would see to that. No one would come looking for a girl lost in the forest, not with a wolf at large. Winter would come, the Riders would protect the village, and everyone would presume she was dead.

"I'll be outside chopping wood." The woman turned to leave. "You should rest. After supper you can tell me what you've decided to do, stay or go." She strode to the door.

"Wait! I have to thank you for your kindness, and I still don't know your name."

The woman looked back over her shoulder. "What has my name got to do with it?"

"A proper thank you always starts with a name," Robyn said, feeling a little silly. "That's what Granny told me."

"Call me Gwen." The door banged shut behind her.

"Well then, I thank you, Gwen," Robyn told the closed door, then lay back down to rest.

The savory smell of meat stew awoke her. The aroma made her realize how hungry she was. She sat up and looked around. Sleep had done wonders for her. She was far less groggy, and her body ached a little less. Across the room a cooking pot hung over the small fireplace; the mouthwatering smell of meat and vegetables wafted over from it. Robyn was ravenous. The woman, Gwen, was not around, yet she must have come back to put the pot on the fire. Robyn felt uncomfortable that she had slept through the visit.

With some effort, she got out of bed and went to stir the stewpot. Being on her feet gave the cabin a whole new perspective. It was tiny, just one room kept snug by the small fire. A wooden table with two chairs stood before the hearth, and Robyn thankfully sank onto the chair nearest the stewpot so she could stir its contents. Standing up made her feel woozy. The bed she'd been sleeping on occupied the far corner but what caught her attention was the rumpled blankets piled up in a makeshift bed behind the door.

The door began to open, and immediately it occurred to her she was wearing only her chemise. It was too late to cover up. The clothes strung up beside the fire were still damp.

"Ah. You've found our dinner," Gwen said.

Robyn was mortified to be sitting in her underwear. "Good evening, ma'am," she said and looked away, her face burning. "I'm sorry not to be presentable."

Gwen gave her a strange look. "Of course you're presentable. If you mean your clothes, then I washed them.

They were covered in blood and mud. I don't think they'll be ready to wear yet. Wait a while for them to dry."

"But what will I wear until then?" Robyn asked, dismayed. This was not how decent young women behaved.

"Are you cold?" Gwen looked doubtful since they were sitting right next to the fire.

"No, but...but I'm not clothed." She was finding the situation hard. Everything was somehow beyond her control.

"Well, you're not naked either." Her gaze was mocking. When Robyn refrained from answering, she sighed. "Put your wet clothes on if you must. But don't come running to me when you get pneumonia." Her sharp response made Robyn feel even more foolish. Then she relaxed. Gwen wasn't like Granny; she wouldn't disapprove of her state of dress. The woman wore trousers for heaven's sake.

She went back to stirring the stew. "How do you take your stew?"

Gwen raised her brow in question.

"Bowl or plate? I shall serve—" She broke off at Gwen's heavy sigh.

Gwen pushed her chair back and reached for the dishes on the shelf beside the fireplace. She pulled a bowl down, went over to the pot and filled it without comment. Then she sat back, took up her spoon and began to eat. Robyn stared at her, not knowing how to respond to such rudeness.

Gwen rolled her eyes and gestured to the pot. "Sit and eat."

Robyn reached for a bowl and filled it awkwardly with her one good hand. Gwen made no move to help; instead she continued to eat noisily.

Robyn dug in, happy to finally have something warm filling her belly.

"So, did you think about it?" Gwen asked, after refilling her bowl for a second helping.

"About what?"

"Staying or leaving," she said. "You will have to stay tonight. We're three hours north of your precious little village, and you'll only get lost if you set out now."

"Three hours?" Robyn asked. "How did you find me? Was it far from here?"

Gwen wiped her mouth with the back of her hand. Robyn thought she heard her mumble, "Questions again," under her breath.

"I was hunting, and you were miles away from the village," Gwen said, instead.

"Was I?" She couldn't remember how far she had run after Hunter's attack, but it certainly had not been miles, had it?

When Gwen did not look like she was going to add to the conversation, Robyn took a deep breath and said, "I would like to stay, at least until my bandages are removed, if you will have me."

"Fine." Gwen went on eating.

Robyn also ate and tried to think of something to keep the conversation going. Her grandmother had taught her to be a good hostess so she wouldn't embarrass Hunter when he entertained at home. She was to be polite, enthusiastic, a beautiful shadow working in the kitchen. Her task was simple, to watch for her husband's cues and be at his side whenever he needed her. With Gwen, it was different. She was a woman, be it a woman who had never enjoyed the training that women in the village had, but she was a woman nevertheless. It should be possible for them to find something to talk about, shouldn't it? She could not act as if Gwen was a man, even if she was strange and wore men's clothes, and lived alone in the forest. Maybe that was the very topic to talk about?

"Are you really living here all by yourself?"

"Aye."

Robyn nodded. Nothing else was forthcoming and after a few minutes she hid her frustration behind another spoonful. The days ahead were going to be long ones.

After supper, Robyn tried to help with the washing up, but Gwen wordlessly took the dishes outside to the water trough. She had also gathered the firewood. It seemed she didn't like anybody interfering in her routine. Robyn sat on the makeshift bed on the floor watching as Gwen rearranged the pillows and blankets on the bed, curious that she made more of a mess than tidying it.

"All right," Gwen said. "Will you need help to get back into bed again?"

"Again?"

"Aye. What do you think happened? You just magically appeared in it?" Gwen snorted and pulled the blanket back. "Get in here, so I can put out the lights."

"I can sleep down here perfectly fine." Robyn patted the blanket on the floor. She was not sure if she could share a bed with a strange woman.

"That is where I sleep," Gwen replied. "We can share if you want?" She broke into a small grin as Robyn rose and headed for the bed wordlessly.

Robyn slipped under the warm covers moving carefully with her injured arm. The room plunged into darkness as Gwen blew out the candle and undressed. Robyn lay listening to the sounds of Gwen preparing for bed. To her surprise, her sight quickly adjusted to the shadows. It was curious how good her eyesight had become recently, but tiredness overcame her before she could give it any more thought.

"Goodnight," she whispered, and receiving no answer fell fast asleep.

The next morning dawned bright and cheerful making it a joy to wake up to. Gwen's bedding lay wadded on the floor, already cold. Granny would have approved of Gwen's early start. A woman should rise with the early birds and do all the chores until midday, and then rest before preparing the perfect dinner for her hard-working husband.

After some fumbling, she managed to get dressed. The bodice was impossible to fasten. It would have to wait until Gwen came back. Dressed in her own clothes she felt almost normal. Normal. Her chest tightened. She slumped onto a chair as the events of last night came flooding back to her.

"But I can't be normal," she whispered aloud. Who else but a crazy woman would put the welfare of a bloodthirsty beast above the will of her betrothed? What had she done?

Now she had no home to go to, no villager with a clear conscience would give her shelter. All the village talk was true, her education had suffered because she'd been raised by Granny, a daft, old woman. Robyn was flawed. Hadn't she seen more in the wolf than a man ever could? Was that even possible for a woman? There was no answer to that.

She put her good hand on the table and pushed herself into a standing position again. She would be as useful as possible to show Gwen that she had made no mistake in saving her. She would bring in more firewood and then make breakfast.

She opened the door to find a huge shadow blocking out the daylight. The wolf stood before her.

Robyn jumped backward and slammed the door shut. She went to bolt it but the stupid thing had no latch. What was that woman thinking, living all alone in the woods and not having a lock on the damn door! Then she remembered Gwen's words that the wolf had done her no harm last night.

"Gwen said I shouldn't fear you," Robyn muttered and tentatively opened the door.

The wolf was gone.

Robyn sighed, not knowing if from relief or disappointment. She went back inside to make the bed. Behind her, the door opened and for a ridiculous moment she thought the wolf had come back. She spun around and found herself eye to eye with a disheveled Gwen. Her hair was uncombed, her clothes were rumpled, and her boots dirty.

"Where have you been? Have you seen it?"

Gwen did not even look at her. Instead, she bent to tie up the laces on her boot. "Are we repeating yesterday?"

"Her, I mean. Have you seen her? The wolf?"

"Aye, she passed by me in the woods. Was she here?"

"Yes." How could she talk about it so matter-of-fact? "You have no latch on your door."

"Aye, what do I need one for?"

"To protect you from the wolf for a start."

"Believe me, lass, I do not need protection."

"I suppose not."

"Explain that, please." That was an unmistakable demand, not a question.

"Well," Robyn gestured with her good hand. "I just mean you don't look like you need anybody's help."

Gwen looked away, combing her fingers through her tousled hair. "Now that you're awake, you can help me with the logs."

"Of course, but could you help me with my bodice first?"

Gwen eyed her, one brow raised. "Are you serious?"

She looked back questioningly. "I can't go outside, looking like this," she explained, running her hand down her belly. "It isn't decent for a woman to not cover herself properly."

"Do you see me wearing one?"

"No, but…aren't you afraid others will talk?"

"I never get any complaints from the squirrels and foxes, but the fishes were strangely quiet the last time I went to the lake."

Robyn pushed the hair back from her face. "Now you're making fun of me."

"Of course I am," Gwen agreed. "Because it is ridiculous to worry what others will say about you out here in the wilderness. Choose your clothes for work, not for beauty."

Robyn looked uncertainly between her bodice and Gwen's shirt and leather vest.

"You won't be cold while you're working. Come on," Gwen said, she was already half out of the door.

"My shoes."

Gwen turned impatiently. "What?"

"I lost one of my shoes in the woods."

She eyed her up and down with such a stern expression that Robyn took a step back. Then Gwen went and rummaged under the bed. She produced a pair of leather boots, not new but well-kept and sturdy. "Put these on," she grumbled, tossing them into Robyn's arms. She wouldn't look at her.

Robyn eyed the boots. "Are those yours?" They looked too small for Gwen's feet.

"Put them on and hurry." She snapped. Gwen was already half out of the door.

Robyn pulled on the boots, glad that at least her feet wouldn't freeze. It wasn't exactly a warm day and snow would be coming soon, but the constant walking between the wood block and the woodpile should keep her warm.

Gwen was a fast and efficient worker. She swung the ax almost as hard as any man Robyn had seen. She had rolled up her sleeves leaving her wiry forearms exposed. The muscles flexed under the skin, her shoulders bunched then released under the rough linen of her shirt. Robyn caught herself watching Gwen instead of piling up the logs. She had to force her gaze away. Her heart beat faster, probably from all the heavy lifting she was doing.

Since she had only one good arm, everything took longer to do, but she did not feel exhausted. Her useless arm didn't hurt if she didn't move it too much. Her legs were strong, and there was not even the slightest twinge in her calf. The wolf bite of a week ago was as good as healed.

"Is she coming by often?" Robyn asked Gwen. She piled more logs into the basket.

"The wolf? From time to time," Gwen answered. "You can never tell when she'll pass through."

Sweat ran down the nape of Robyn's neck, cooling her spine. She could wait to see the wolf again but the need to clean her body was urgent. "You said something about a lake, is it close by?"

"Why? Are you trying to make a map of my place?" Gwen growled.

"No." Robyn hurried to assure her. "I wouldn't know the first thing about that. I'm only a woman. It's not my place to explore lands."

Apparently Gwen hadn't expected this explanation. She shook her head, grabbing her ax in one hand placing a log onto the block with the other. "When the time comes to take you back to your village I will bind your eyes. Just in case you should rise above your station and begin to memorize a thing or two, after all."

Robyn didn't think she'd be going back to the village anytime soon. Hunter had warned her to run as far away as she could. And that's exactly what she'd do.

"Lass, pay attention," Gwen said, snapping her out of her thoughts.

"Huh?"

"Why do you want to know about the lake?"

"We need to get cleaned up?" Robyn was mystified she even had to explain it.

Setting the ax aside, Gwen took a long hard look at her. She turned her attention to her dirty hands and rolled her tight shoulders.

"Fine," she said and turned to go. Robyn stood by the log pile uncertain what to do.

"Are you coming?" Gwen asked impatiently, only slowing down a little.

"But you just said—"

"Hurry up or stay dirty." Gwen marched on, and Robyn had to run to catch up with her, surprised the cut on her foot wasn't hurting anymore. Her limp had disappeared, and she'd only noticed now? She followed Gwen deeper into the woods where no sunlight penetrated the trees, and the air was much colder. Gwen walked on, unaffected by the cold and Robyn stumbled along beside her.

A nearby bush rattled loudly, and she leaped back in fright, treading on Gwen's foot. She waited, expecting a curse, or to be scolded; instead found herself maneuvered behind Gwen's board back where she felt immediately safer. Together they watched a squirrel emerge from the bush with a nut grasped between its claws.

"A little jumpy, aren't we?" Gwen said dryly though she kept her grip on Robyn's wrist.

Robyn watched the squirrel bound away. This time she refused to feel foolish. It could have been anything hiding in that bush. Snakes, a wild boar, maybe even the wolf?

"Is it far to the lake?" she asked instead. "Do other people go there?"

Gwen raised an eyebrow at her. "It's more a pool than a lake and we'll only be sharing it with the animals." She rubbed her hand along Robyn's cold arm. "You're freezing. Come on, it's just behind the trees and down the hill a little way."

"All right." Robyn was glad. This part of the forest unnerved her. At best, it was so remote nobody would come along and surprise them. Hunter would never come here. She shivered with a mixture of the cold and the unpleasantness of his memory. Gwen's leather vest found its way around her shoulders bathing her in the warmth of her body. It was so big she could drape it around her like a cape. She looked over at Gwen. "But aren't you cold?"

Gwen shrugged. "If you'd move a little faster, lass, you wouldn't be cold either."

It was a beautiful pool. Partly hidden by the trees and undergrowth, but open enough to the skies for sunlight to sparkle across the jade green water. It was a quiet and tranquil place, with ferns and smooth wet rocks feathering its banks. It wasn't so far away from the cabin, and Gwen told her she could come back anytime and bathe on her own if she wished to.

The water was too cold to bathe properly, but by dipping her arms into the water and cleaning her face Robyn felt fresh again. Gwen splashed water on her face and neck washing the sweat and grime away from her throat.

The sun was dipping below the tree line, so they turned back toward the cabin. The wind whistled through the trees, stealing the last dry leaves from the branches and shaking the massive crowns of the fir trees. Above them, thick gray clouds were forming a storm front. Robyn peeked a sideways look at Gwen walking beside her. Her wet hair was tugged behind her ears. She didn't care that her hair was soaking wet on a freezing day. Robyn had been more careful with hers. In the village, a girl's hair was a signature of her beauty. It should be a treat for her husband's eyes. The air rushed from her lungs at a sudden memory.

She stopped short and blinked up at the overcast sky. Three weeks from now she would have become a wife. Hunter's wife. Now she was here, in the woods, feeling more comfortable with this sour, strange woman than she ever had with him. Why was that? Was it because that same stranger had taken her in, fed her, and warmed her? Was it because Gwen had not left her in the woods to die?

Fear and anger churned at her stomach, and she hugged herself with both arms, even her bad arm moved to wrap around her. Robyn looked down in surprise at her bandaged arm. It moved freely and without pain. It was as if her injury had never happened. She bent and flexed it in wonder, moving it up, then down, then rotating it in small circles.

"What are you doing?" Gwen was smiling at her contortions.

"It doesn't hurt at all," Robyn answered, mystified. Then Gwen's hands were on her, removing the bandage and gently probing the smooth skin with skillful fingers.

"Looks like you're healing," she said and shrugged. To Robyn's ears, her indifference sounded forced.

"Right." She was too awed for any other response. There was no explanation for it. Her arm was healed when she'd expected it to take weeks to get better.

They strode on in silence as the gloom gathered around them.

"What were you thinking of back there?" Gwen suddenly asked. Robyn looked at her. Was she so obvious?

"I…I…" She didn't know how to put it in words. What had happened to her? What had happened with Hunter? "Well, my wedding was supposed to take place in a few weeks—"

"So you want to go back now?" Gwen cut her short before Robyn had a chance to finish.

"No!" she blurted in alarm. "I couldn't." Her voice became steady. "I crossed the path of the wolf and chased it away before the Riders could hurt her."

Gwen stared at her. "And now you pity yourself for not presenting her on a silver platter for those killers."

"Of course not!" Robyn objected. She was becoming angry. "You said I shouldn't fear the wolf and I believe you. I wanted to protect her."

"What now?" Gwen asked.

"Now I can never go back," Robyn said. It was the simple truth.

Gwen was silent. She kicked at a stone with the toe of her boot and eyed Robyn skeptically. Robyn had just declared she prized the well-being of a creature of the forest over the diktats of the village.

She could never go back to the village and ask forgiveness. Hunter hated her. She had sided with the wolf. She wasn't sure why, but it had shown mercy to both her and Hunter when he had fainted. Surely it was only justice to show mercy back? But the famous Captain Wolfmounter would never see it like that. He would aim his arrows at her, and he wouldn't miss a second time.

A snowflake hit her square on the nose. She looked up to a sky filled with fluffy, falling snowflakes. They stuck to her hair and her eyelashes and made her smile.

"Winter is here," Gwen whispered next to her. Then she tilted her head back to catch the snowflakes on her tongue. She smiled. "You should stay here while it lasts."

Chapter 6

WHITNEY LOOKED RIDICULOUS IN HER monstrous dress of pink satin. The white roses bedecking her hair underscored her fragile beauty, as she liked to point out to anybody who would listen. Unfortunately, it was Rose who had to weave every single bloom into her sister's hair.

At first Rose hadn't realized what was going on. She had come home three days ago and, to her trepidation, found Hunter talking to her father in their living room. Was he complaining about her going to Spindlefinger's inn that night? Whitney pulled her into the kitchen; she was excited almost to the point of swooning. She told Rose that the great, the perfect, the most handsome, most desirable man in all the village was at that very moment asking their father for her hand! Rose managed to not get the ax from the wood shed and chase the bastard off the premises. Instead, she remembered what she and Greta had agreed about not being too obvious, and stayed silent.

And, as a reward for her calm manner and good sense, here she was, arranging the veil around her sister's face. How absurd it all was! A few days ago, she had her plan all figured out. She would wake these brain-dead women from their trances. But it had all gone so terribly wrong. Instead of standing by her side, Robyn had abandoned her. Rose refused to believe Hunter's flimsy tale that the wolf had killed her. The white wolf would not kill a beautiful thing like Robyn. Nevertheless, Robyn was gone, and Rose's plan was in tatters. Now all she could do was give into Greta's pleas to behave herself. So, instead of opening eyes and minds, she was a bridesmaid at her sister and her enemy's wedding, playing her role as nicely as she possibly could.

Her hands attached the last rose to her sister's hair while her eyes lingered on the treetops under the slowly sinking sun. Through the open window, she could hear the chatter from their guests down in the garden where the ceremony would take place this evening. Since Darwin Prospector was the eldest male in the village, he was to wed the couple. He would have done so for Hunter and Robyn, and now he was doing it for his own daughter. Not with the pride of a father seeing his child become a woman, but with the relief of an old man who had finally gotten rid of one of his girls. Rose sighed and checked her handiwork one last time. "I think we're done."

Whitney watched herself in the mirror, her eyes filling with tears. "Oh, I am blessed," she murmured with quivering lips.

"If you'd only been blessed with brains," Rose muttered under her breath. How she would love to get away from here like Robyn had, but she didn't want to give up her fight so easily. Her ideas were good; she just had to wait until the uproar the wolf had caused subsided and then start anew.

Whitney grabbed her arm with cold hands. "Do you think I will make him proud?" she asked wide-eyed.

"He chose you above all the others, so he must see something in you." Rose considered that a diplomatic answer. One of the many reasons she was so determined to succeed was her fury at seeing her sister fit in so easily into this world of men. She accepted her inferior place without question, and never looked beyond the given path of daughter, wife, and mother. With a little help, Rose had considered Whitney as capable of thinking for herself as Rose was. Now, with this marriage, she was losing heart.

"I swear I will try my best to please him," Whitney said. "And who knows, we might conceive our first son tonight. How delightful! Imagine if I were to fulfill my duty so fast. I would be respected and congratulated by the whole village."

Whitney looked so ridiculously happy that Rose felt sorry for her. Hunter was a bastard, and he would not shrink from getting physical if Whitney failed to obey his orders. On the other hand, her sister was the most pliable woman in the village. She'd readily obey and meet the needs of her husband.

The other problem Rose was facing was that this wedding had turned the heads of the villagers. No one had given a second thought about Robyn. Hunter had told them all his sob story and who was there to doubt him?

"Well then," Rose said and took a deep breath. "You are ready to meet your husband."

"I'll be down in a minute," Whitney answered, taking that minute to examine herself from head to toe in the mirror. "You must make sure he's in place. Our marriage will never be a happy one if he sees me in my wedding dress before we meet at the altar."

"If that's the only reason your marriage won't be happy, I'm glad," Rose said and went to the door.

The house was alive with people. People who had never come to visit after their mother had died. Mostly for fear their children might become infected with whatever it was that had turned Rose into such a deviant girl. Now half of the village was gathered inside their cottage, the remainder spilling out into the garden.

Rose was making her way downstairs when cold fingers closed around her upper arm, pulling her violently aside into a quiet hallway. Hunter faced her, not slackening his grip. He was dressed in fine white linen with his hair drawn back by a band of leather. She was stunned that he had dragged her away like that, and in her own home. His dark eyes flashed with anger.

"We may be among friends now," he hissed, "but don't think I'm not watching your every move, you sour-faced little bitch."

She pulled her arm free and glared at him. Despite her promise to Greta, she was unable to keep her mouth shut. "And maybe I'll watch you right back," she spat out.

He regarded her coldly for a second. She could see him processing her words carefully. "You're pretty brazen for a girl in your position." His mouth twisted into a sneer.

"And what position would that be?" She refused to back down. He was no more than a cheat and a liar, and she would find out the truth about Robyn no matter what.

"I will be a brother to you in a few minutes—"

"You will be *nothing* to me," she hissed.

He clenched his jaw. "Oh, I expect to be everything to you, sweetheart." She refused to give him the satisfaction of seeing her shudder. Instead she chose to attack.

"Like you hoped to be everything to Robyn?"

He sucked in a sharp breath. "I tried my best to bring her back safely," he answered through gritted teeth. His earlier show of remorse evaporated when she alone was the audience. "Robyn is dead, and you should be grateful I'm here to keep you all safe."

Rose pursed her lips. He was always going to stick to his hero's story. "You only keep yourself safe, Wolfmounter. Always have, always will."

She looked him square in the eye, seeing the sweat beading on his temple. His neck was red with fury. He raised his hand to slap her. "Your father was too lenient with you. Proper punishment is what you need. And let me tell you, once you are under my—"

"Ah, there you are, Captain." Hans barreled down the hall toward them, and the conversation halted. Hunter turned to greet him. Hans smiled politely at Rose and shook Hunter's hand with too much enthusiasm. "Such a beautiful day for a wedding."

She eyed him skeptically, as usual the buffoon had timed his appearance badly. The conversation with Wolfmounter had just been getting interesting.

"Prospector said the ceremony can begin as soon as you're ready," Hans said.

"Then I'd better get back to Whitney." Rose took the opportunity to squeeze by them and hurry away. Her behavior would not go unpunished, but for the moment it was worth her father's anger to tell Hunter what she thought of him.

"Rose," Greta hissed and waved her over to the back door. She looked anything but pleased. "Didn't I tell you to watch your mouth?"

"I tried, but he's such a bully. Who wouldn't have lost their temper?"

"Every right raised girl in the village."

"Everyone knows I'm the insane one. I'm the witch. What's the worst that can happen? Maybe they'll abandon me in the forest like he did Robyn?"

"There are worse things," Greta said quietly and gazed over Rose's shoulder. Rose managed to bite her tongue in time. Her friend was a strong woman, intelligent, and independent, but since Robyn had gone missing, Greta had become more worried and less confident. She tried to fit in more often than she tried to rebel. Once, in the time of the Black Wolf, Greta had been like Rose, but now every failure seemed to grind down her spirit. Rose realized Greta did not need her haranguing her, at least not today.

"Have you heard anything from Robyn, yet?"

Greta shook her head. "No, but I haven't made it far enough into the woods to investigate anything."

Rose sighed, Greta was the only one she could talk to, and they were both convinced Robyn was not dead. "And Hans knows nothing?"

"Even if my brother knew something, do you really think he would talk to me about it? He worships Wolfmounter, and I wouldn't be one bit surprised if he took the blame for anything his glorious captain did."

"We need to ask more questions."

Greta shook her head in exasperation. "I should have never told you about the Black Wolf."

"What was there to tell?" Rose asked, barely keeping her voice down. "I was there. I was bitten. And after that it was easy to solve the puzzle on my own."

"It all went so wrong the first time," Greta whispered, her eyes downcast.

Rose took her hand. "I didn't mean to lose my temper. It's just that I can't bear it any longer; the blankness in their eyes, so dull, so hollow."

Greta looked smaller somehow with her slumped shoulders, and waxy, pale skin. She nodded, more to herself than to Rose. "I know," she said. "By bringing the wolf into the village I wanted to change their situation, but my recklessness only doomed those I loved."

"You didn't doom me." Rose tried to soothe her. That drew a sad laugh from Greta.

"No. Not you, Rose, just every other woman," she said, gesturing around them.

Maybe Greta's plans hadn't worked out the way she'd hoped, but she had laid the foundation for Rose's work. The Black Wolf had opened her eyes, and she was determined to continue Greta's plans to fulfillment. "My ideas were good, Greta, I hadn't considered the possibility that Robyn might not come to me first."

Greta held her head high now, staring directly at Rose. Her eyes swam with unshed tears. "Then your idea wasn't good enough," she said, angrily. "You could have waited. We could have thought up something together, but you went ahead and—"

"Waited? For what? For how long? We have done *nothing* all these years," Rose cut in, her heart hammering in her chest. "And now we are all at marriageable age, and what next when we are lumbered with husbands and children?" She was caught between wanting to shake some sense into her friend or pull her into her arms to comfort her and apologize for her harsh words. "Robyn needed the herbs." She tried to explain her reasoning. "It was an opportunity I couldn't pass up. And just to set things straight, I didn't want to do what you did. My plan was to get them one after another, and that alone would have taken me months if not years. So don't tell me I should have waited any longer."

"And what do you have now?" Greta said, her lips thin and pale. "Hunter will be part of your family. You will be under his command."

Rose blinked. This was the second time in a few minutes she had been warned about this. First by Hunter and now Greta. Was she missing a clue somewhere? What did it matter he would be her brother? She would be safely in charge of her father's household, well away from Hunter Wolfmounter and his wheeling and dealing. Before she could speak, Hans appeared at his sister's side, sliding his arm around her. She stood up straighter.

"Greta, I thought you'd be outside with the other guests?" he said, in a gentle but determined way.

Rose bit back an angry retort. Greta merely nodded consent, gave Rose a look that could have meant anything, and went out to the garden without a word.

"You and your sister should count yourselves lucky." Hans turned his attention to Rose.

"I wouldn't quite put it that way, but I'm merely a girl and can't possibly see the big picture."

Hans took a step towards her, his face full of eagerness. "Captain Wolfmounter only has the best in mind for you. You will see how good he is at taking care of his new family after the wedding." He smiled at her. "I'm looking forward to seeing you at the party at Spindlefinger's tonight." Hans went out after his sister leaving Rose to go back upstairs to Whitney. Hunter passed her at the foot of the stairs, his eyes narrowed, jaw set.

In the last light rays of sunset, Whitney fought her way to the head of the stairs in her puffy pink dress.

"Is everyone outside?" she asked Rose anxiously.

"Everyone is waiting for you," Rose announced, and reached out her hand to guide the bride to her future husband.

Spindlefinger's inn was full of laughter, music, and dance. Rose had not been to many parties; the Prospectors were not the kind of family people invited along to their special events. One daughter had the manners of a witch, and the other, though a beauty, suffered because of her sister's eccentric behavior. If the family had been rich then maybe some young man might have taken a chance on the pretty one, but the Prospectors weren't, and so Whitney languished. Until now. Now, she had landed the best catch in the village.

Rose stood to one side and watched her sister dance with the man she would have to call brother now. Well, she would call him something, he could be sure of that! She did not feel a loss that Whitney was moving out. They had never been close even though they were twins. Whitney had always accepted her duties and took pleasure in them. She thrilled at any praise or attention their father might casually drop for her hard work in the kitchen. Rose was renowned for holding the opposite point of view.

"A toast to my wife!" Hunter yelled, raising his glass. Rose couldn't see Greta anywhere. Hans had done well in keeping them separate.

"Dearest Kidne...Kitty," he started and Whitney giggled and clung to his arm. "You have tamed the Wolfmounter. I am honored to have you for my wife and the mother of my future sons."

Everyone applauded, and Rose took a sip from her cup of beer to wash down her rising bile. She wanted to vomit all over Hunter's shining boots. Her sister smiled, reveling in her certain knowledge that every unmarried girl in the room dreamed of swapping places with her. Rose let the nitwit dream; she was more than content to be left behind to look after her father.

As if thinking of him brought him to her notice, Rose saw her father and Robyn's Grandmother deep in conversation on the other side of the room. She slunk over to the table of wedding presents and pretended to read the labels while eavesdropping on them.

"Oh Darwin, you have honored me with this invitation to your daughter's wedding. Especially after everything that has happened."

"It was the least I could do. You were so kind to provide the dress rather than make me pay out for another one."

"It wasn't of any use for me after...after Robyn left. It felt like the right thing to do. I wanted to contribute something to the wedding. I'm so glad that everything went well for Whitney."

"Bless the good Captain. He has been kind to both of us."

"I bless him every night, my friend, every night." Granny sighed. "I feared I could never show my face again after Robyn ran away and was killed. The Captain was so generous, and he forgave me for the unruly girl I raised."

"He offered for Whitney mostly to make sure Spindlefinger would not be left with the cost of a canceled wedding."

"Such a saint."

"Definitely."

Rose was furious. Even Granny hadn't shed a tear over Robyn. She was celebrating as if this wedding had not originally been planned for her lost granddaughter. The night Robyn went missing, Rose had been on the way to their cottage. She had done this every night since Robyn had been bitten, always hoping to witness any change in her behavior. She had not seen Robyn run away, but she had heard Granny curse her wastrel granddaughter. Rose realized it had finally happened and hurried home to wait. She had been certain Robyn would come to her first, but the Riders had stopped her on the way and she learned Robyn had followed the wolf instead.

She needed fresh air. Rose began to make her way through the crowd when behind her the Bell of Night rang out. She stopped and turned around reluctantly. There was no point in slipping out now.

"My beloved son," her father said. His bony hand grasped Hunter's shoulder and gave his daughter a slight bow with his head. "And Whitney, my darling daughter. I know you will be an exceptional wife to this man who has endured so much these past days. Not many years ago, he killed the Black Wolf and saved our village from falling victim to that evil beast. I can't begin to say how proud I am to call him family. May you both be blessed with a boy child tonight!"

It was the ritual father's blessing, and the crowd applauded and cheered. A couple of Red Riders howled like wolves for their captain and raised their glasses to him.

Rose hid her disgust best as she could. The feast was over and the wedding night was to begin. Her father went first, parting the crowd as the couple followed him to the door. Spindlefinger ceremoniously held the door open for them. All three of them came to a halt right next to her. Her father drew himself up proudly, turned to her and smiled.

"I may be losing two daughters tonight," he said, "but I'm gaining the best son a father could dream of."

Rose fixed her father with a stare, what was he talking about? Then she became aware of the nasty grin on Hunter's face.

"No," she whispered, the truth dawning.

Her father took her by the wrist and guided her towards Hunter's waiting hand. He grabbed for her, but she pulled out of reach.

"I grant you service in my household, Rose Prospector, because I cannot bear to separate you and your dear sister after so many years of caring for each other. You will live under my roof and help my wife with her domestic duties. This is my wedding present for my darling Kitty."

Rose just looked at him, her mouth agape. Whitney came over and threw her arms around her neck. "Oh, I'm so happy! I couldn't wait to tell you, but Hunter said we must keep it a secret to make the surprise so much better for you." She pulled away, her teeth flashing in a big, happy smile. Then she kissed Rose on both cheeks.

Rose's head spun. She felt nauseous. She was torn between running away or jumping on him and clawing his smug face to shreds. How dare he? She would never come with him! With her jaw set, she looked over to her father. "What shall become of my father if there's nobody left to care for him?"

"Don't worry about me, child," Darwin padded her cold cheek. "Granny will look out for me. She cooks and cleans, and has offered to help run my house."

Her eyes darted over to the old woman who gave her a bold stare.

"Now go with them, Rose," her father prompted, pushing her gently towards the door.

She wanted to scream but her heart was hard, like ice, there was no real surprise in their betrayal after all. Just the residual disappointment that everyone was so stupid they didn't even know they were playing into Hunter's hands. Why did he want her under his control? Was he planning to kill her? She would flee the first chance she got, even if she had to hide out in the woods.

And then the real hurt hit her. Greta had known about this all along. It explained her strange behavior before the wedding. Greta, her one and only friend, had abandoned her, just as Robyn had. She was alone in this fight. There was no one left who cared for her anymore.

Hunter grabbed her arm so hard it hurt while Whitney linked arms with him on his other side. Hunter Wolfmounter walked out of Spindlefinger's inn into the crisp snowy air with a satisfied grin on his face and both Prospector daughters at his service, for as long as he cared for either of them.

Chapter 7

Gwen rolled her eyes. Robyn noticed she did that a lot. And she mostly did it when Robyn tried to be useful. For Gwen nothing was ever good enough. She didn't cook with enough spices, she didn't wake up early enough, and she couldn't get their clothes clean enough. How could she, when Gwen came home each evening looking like a pig fresh from a mud wallow?

She was a hard woman to please, and Robyn suspected she didn't want to be pleased at all. She was dissatisfied with everything Robyn had been taught as essential for a village girl to do. And then there were the long winter evenings. If Gwen was home at all, she was silent and brooding. They ate in silence; they went to bed in silence, and they looked out of different windows in silence. Robyn never knew what to say, and Gwen made no effort either. Robyn began to feel unwelcome.

"Gwen?" Robyn asked one night. Three days of snow had covered the cabin up to its windowsills. "Do you want me to leave?"

The silence was interrupted only by the crackling of the wood burning in the fire. Robyn looked at Gwen who seemed mesmerized by the colors in the flames. "Go if you want to," she answered indifferently. "Good luck with the snow."

Robyn sighed in frustration. "I don't want to leave," she clarified. "But I don't think you want me here. I can't seem to do anything right, so all I'm doing is eating your food and using your bed with nothing to offer in exchange."

"You could learn to be useful, but if you'd rather give up already…" Gwen shrugged. "You know how to get back to the village." She didn't look away from her fire gazing.

"I *don't*. And I couldn't go even if I wanted to—Hey! What do you mean I could learn to be useful?" Robyn narrowed her eyes. "What have I been doing these last couple of days? I tried to do my chores to your satisfaction, but you're never happy."

"Where you satisfied with your work?"

Robyn was surprised with the question. She thought about it for a second and answered, "Yes."

"Okay, so what do you need my approval for?"

"I…" Robyn bit her lip. "I was raised that way. A woman needs to be told if she did good or not, how else will she know if her work is satisfactory?"

Gwen still didn't look at her, but Robyn thought she saw the corner of her mouth twitch. "So what have you just told me when I asked what you thought about your own work?"

"I said I did it to my liking," Robyn answered hesitantly. "So you were never disappointed?"

Gwen rolled her eyes, again.

"Stop doing that! It makes me feel more stupid than I actually am."

"You're not stupid, lass."

Robyn was stunned. That was the nicest thing Gwen had ever said to her.

Robyn chose to stay. She went ahead with the chores when Gwen wasn't there, glad provisions had been made for the long winter ahead. She did what she could with the wood pile, but she was slow. She did take the basket into the forest, though never too far from the cabin and searched for small twigs and branches for kindling. It was good to be of any use at all while Gwen provided their food and did...things out in the woods. Robyn didn't know where she went each day and didn't dare ask. She didn't want to hear anything she might not like. Maybe Gwen bought the rabbits and partridges she brought home for supper from some nearby farmer? All Robyn knew was she never had any hunting gear with her. Not that she was awake when Gwen left in the morning. The woman moved as quiet as a mouse. In the past weeks, Robyn had never once seen her sleeping on the makeshift bed on the floor. She was already fast asleep when Gwen went to bed, and still asleep when she left in the early dawn.

It was time to wash their bed linen again. It hadn't been done for a couple of days now. Oh, how angry Granny would be, if she saw the state the house was in! They couldn't think of inviting a man inside, not with blankets on the floor and the dishes not dried.

Robyn blinked, dropping twigs into her basket. She had never thought of a man coming here, not once. She doubted that a male person had ever laid eyes on Gwen's little refuge. But she was sure that there had been somebody once, even though Gwen never said a word about it. She cast a glance behind her and took in the view for a second. The cabin was small. It had one door and three windows, a thatched roof with a stone chimney. How could a single woman build—The snow creaked behind her. She twisted around and found herself eye to eye with the wolf. With a choked cry, she fell back and slipped onto her backside. The kindling tumbled from her basket.

The wolf sat back on her hindquarters. Her blue eyes shone with the glow of the snow all around them. Slowly, so as not to alarm it, Robyn turned her head to gauge the distance to the cabin. The wolf growled. Then she did a curious thing, she lifted her paw and pressed it down into the snow, repeating the motion. Curiosity pushed away Robyn's initial fear. She remembered Gwen's words and she found she believed them. This wolf was no beast, and she would harm neither Robyn nor Gwen. If anything, she was a friend.

"Well, hello friend," she said softly.

The wolf lowered her head as if nodding, and then she came closer. Robyn's heartbeat increased, but she tried to stay as still as possible. When the wolf stopped, she was only inches away from her, both paws buried in the snow. Her head was low, inviting.

Robyn lifted her hand towards the big white head and started stroking the warm fur between the she-wolf's ears. A soft growl was her reward. The wolf didn't seem to mind her cold fingers. She lay down a little so Robyn could reach more of her, and Robyn did so gladly. The wolf's nearness warmed her; she radiated a calm that made Robyn's insides tingle. She felt safe here, in the middle of the dark woods, deep in the winter's snow scratching an enormous wolf between its ears. Bemused, Robyn thought about it. This was the first time she had been away from home. And here she was, far away from her village with just a wolf to keep her company, and no men and no Granny to tell her what to do every waking hour of the day. She realized she felt happier in this moment than she did the day Hunter told her she would be his wife.

Now Hunter was gone, and she was tickling the ears of his enemy. She started giggling. The furry ears moved under her fingers, interested in the sound.

"Oh dear, I'm so glad they didn't catch you." Robyn put both her hands on either side of the warm face and looked into the blue eyes. "Those killers will never find you. We are here to protect you. Gwen won't have to watch out for you alone, not while I'm here."

The wolf stared back, and the next thing she knew, a heavy, wet tongue was sliding a warm trail up her face. She wrinkled her nose and shook her head. "Someone needs to brush her teeth." Without thinking, Robyn grabbed a hand full of snow and rubbed it playfully onto the wolf's snout.

The wolf stared at her, and for a second she thought she had made a terrible mistake. Then the big bad wolf sneezed and brushed her paw over her muzzle to free it from the snow. Robyn laughed and set her basket aside.

"You should see yourself, afraid of a little snow," she said. The wolf jumped on her in a blink. She fell backward and soft paws rolled her on into the drift, deeper and deeper. She laughed, a happy, heartfelt sound that she couldn't stop. Her skin started prickling from the cold snow; her hair was wet and her underskirts were clinging to her shivering legs and she couldn't have cared less.

Two or three times she tried to free herself. The wolf jumped backward long enough for Robyn to scramble to her feet and attempt to run. She grabbed a handful of snow to throw at the wolf as she closed in on her heels. They ran around the cabin, slipping and sliding. The wolf growled happily, wagging her tail and jumping all around her. At the cabin's door, Robyn stopped to catch her breath. Her fingers were frozen. The tips of them burned as she combed through the thick warm pelt. The wolf licked her wrist and bumped her nose against Robyn's ribs.

"Will you come inside with me?" she asked, one hand already on the door knob. "I'll start a fire for the both of us."

The wolf nudged her again then turned to leave. Robyn paused. "Will you come back again?" she called. The wolf stopped in her tracks and turned around and seemed almost to nod before she vanished back into the woods.

Robyn knelt before the fireplace. Her hands were shivering so hard she barely managed to click the firestones together. She was frozen to the bone and still she couldn't stop the grin on her face as she sat on the floor staring at the stones in her white hands. Behind her, the door swung open, and Gwen came in, bringing the north wind with her. She had Robyn's basket in her hand.

"I suppose this is yours?" she asked, with no greeting, no smile. Robyn grinned back at her. "What now? Are you daydreaming of your prince coming to rescue you?"

"I don't need to be rescued." Robyn took back her basket. Gwen raised an eyebrow. Excited to tell Gwen of her encounter she burst out, "The wolf was here again. We had a snowball fight!"

Gwen burst out laughing and went over to the fireplace. "You played in the snow with a dangerous beast and stand there telling me about it, all full of yourself."

The smile slipped from Robyn's lips. "Should I feel guilty?" The wolf was the enemy, except she wasn't.

Gwen shrugged, snatched the stones from Robyn's cold fingers and lit the fire, blowing on the small flames to help them catch. "I can't tell you how to feel, lass."

"Because you're not a man."

"Because I can't see inside your head," she answered harshly. "If you listen to yourself, what do you hear?"

"My heartbeat."

Gwen's shoulders sank.

Robyn closed her eyes and tried again. "I feel warm and happy and satisfied." She had to smile as she remembered the look the wolf had given her after the first snowy, surprise attack.

"And that's good?"

"Very."

"So why not leave it at that?"

"Because—" She sneezed.

Gwen rose from the fire to face her. Robyn thought she saw the ghost of a smile on her lips, but wasn't sure. "Let's get you warm, lass. Who knows when the wolf will be back to play?" Gwen nodded towards the fire and Robyn went over and warmed her freezing fingers.

"Turn."

She did so and felt fingers at the nape of her dress. Startled she spun around, nearly stepping back into the flames. Gwen pulled her away from it. "Careful you don't burn, lass."

"What are you doing?"

"Helping you get undressed. You're freezing, and your clothes are wet. Take them off and I'll get a warm blanket." Gwen tried to sound reasonable, but her face betrayed her impatience.

Robyn stepped aside. The nape of her neck tingled where Gwen had touched her. "You can't just undress me in public," she said, trying to sort out the queer feelings in her belly.

"In public?" Gwen snorted. "Lass, I've seen you in your undergarments enough times. Now don't make a fuss and get undressed."

Robyn didn't make a move. Her cheeks felt hot and her lips dry. Gwen gave her a strange look, and Robyn didn't understand that either, but just the thought of being this close to Gwen in only her undergarments made her feel uncomfortable. No, not uncomfortable; more like nervous. "I...um, I can get undressed myself, thank you."

Gwen shrugged. "I was only helping with the first button."

"Well, if you were my husband you could undress me, but you are merely a friend, and this is inappropriate." Robyn didn't know where that had come from, and the look of hurt on Gwen's face didn't help her to think clearly either. She only knew that in the village she had lived by rules, she had known what to do and what not to do, out here came new territory with new rules. She couldn't trust her feelings, she didn't know how to behave to please. It was stupid to think about all that now, but at least knowing what to do made her stop questioning herself.

"I don't know what you see in me," Robyn finally confessed. "What do you want from me? Back in the village there were rules—"

Gwen stomped her foot and the wooden floor creaked. "I'm not a man of your village. I don't make rules for you. And I'm not willing to use you as a slave in my house. Heavens, I thought we'd gone beyond this stupid discussion."

Robyn looked down at her feet; she couldn't meet those cold blue eyes. Gwen took a deep breath.

"Listen, I've had enough of this. You're mixing up worlds here, lass, and you should try and think about what you have here and what you had down in the village. If you want to go back, then go. If you want to stay, then stay. But do not expect me to act like one of them. Up here you will take care of yourself, and no man will be above you. Think about it, and in the morning tell me your decision. I'll be back for it."

She brushed past Robyn and pushed out through the door into the snow-filled night.

Morning came, and Robyn sat on the blankets on the floor. Her fingers pressed against the rough fabric. She was angry that she could not make a final decision. Maybe there was a small chance of forgiveness if she went pleading back to the village and accepted whatever punishment the men saw fit for her. Whatever she had done wrong, would Hunter still want to kill her? The image of an arrow missing her by mere inches leaped into her mind. Hunter had stood not five feet away from her, aiming right for her.

Her throat tightened painfully, and she couldn't breathe for a second. Her hands flew to her sternum, pressing against her chest in panic. Air! She needed air! She scrambled to her feet and made for the door. With one hard tug, she pulled it open and took a long, deep breath. The crisp air pinched at her lungs and put the life back into her. With huge gulps, she sucked in the taste of freedom and let her eyes sting with tears from the cold.

It was stupid to think Hunter wouldn't kill her given the chance. He would cut her throat just like he had done with the Black Wolf; Robyn was in no doubt about it. And it was even sillier to think of the she-wolf as a beast, she was nothing like that, she was a friendly creature, and Robyn enjoyed her company. The wolf had never done Robyn any harm. She had never done anyone harm, and no man had the right to kill her because they imagined a threat where none existed. Robyn knew that now, but she felt there was so much more still to know. So much she would never have the chance to learn if she went back to the village. Finally, her thoughts were clear, and she nearly sobbed with relief that she was here, free in the forest, instead of a village girl married to Hunter. Gwen was right, here no man would be above her, and maybe that was what she had always wanted.

Robyn heard the wolf approach from a distance. She had smelled her from afar and swore she felt her heartbeat fall into a different rhythm as if to match the wolf's with her own. Was that why she could breathe so easily out here? The wolf, her wolf, was coming closer, and its presence calmed her.

"I'm so glad you came," she whispered when it appeared, a smile danced across her lips. The wolf did not look up, so Robyn had to crouch in front of her and put both her hands on the furry face. "Thank you."

She stroked the fluffy ears and placed a kiss on her wet nose.

"With you here, the decision is easy." Blue eyes met hers and Robyn shivered involuntarily. This time she was prepared and pulled away before the wolf's wet, rough tongue could reach her cheek.

"I'm not that witless," she said, and pulling up her skirts dashed off into the woods toward the lake. Snow still lay heavy under the trees. She ran through drifts of it, wetting her legs. She did not feel the cold, she just felt ecstasy pumping through her veins. The wolf ran alongside her, sometimes jumping in front of her. She tripped, and both of them went rolling.

Robyn opened her eyes to find the wolf on top of her panting fast and looking very pleased with herself. She pulled her hand free to wipe away a splash of mud from the white fur of her forehead.

The wolf grunted.

"Are you mocking me?" she asked. "This…" She pointed at her supine position, "is indecorous. And a woman should never look indecorous."

The wolf actually rolled her eyes! Robyn was sure of it.

"You need to behave yourself, young lady," she said imitating Granny's scolding voice. Suddenly, she grabbed a handful of muddy snow and smeared the bright white fur. The wolf wailed in protest and jumped away. Robyn laughed and sat up to look around.

"That is what I would call a public display of indecency." Robyn tried to stand on wobbly legs. The ground was slippery, and it only took the slightest nudge from a wet nose for her to fall back down again. She grabbed another handful of mud to throw. The wolf yipped and jumped on her. Together they rolled around in the dirt with Robyn enjoying herself more than ever. It was the most playful, unladylike thing she had ever done in her entire life. She had never, not even as a child, played like that, rolling and laughing and not worrying about getting dirty.

Finally, the wolf nuzzled her a farewell and disappeared into the trees. Robyn was exhausted, mud covered, and not in the least unhappy about her situation. Instead, she went about getting water for a hot bath.

Robyn would have loved to soak in the tub longer, but she was too tired to carry more than two buckets of water from the lake up to the cabin. She washed the mud from her body and knelt before the tub in her chemise to wash her hair.

She smelled Gwen before she set foot in the cabin. The door opened, and the heavy footfall of boots sounded on the wooden floor. They stopped next to the tub. Robyn looked up. Gwen was as disheveled and grim as always;

the leather vest lay open and her shirt was creased and crumpled. Her trousers were filthy with mud. Her blond hair was pinned behind her ears, pushed back more for comfort than for beauty. She crossed her arms and she looked sternly down at Robyn. Not breaking eye contact, Robyn reached for a towel and threw it. Gwen grabbed it more out of reflex than anything.

"You still got mud on your neck from our little quarrel by the lake," Robyn said and turned back to the tub. There was a sharp intake of breath.

"About time you realized." Gwen's tone was flat.

Robyn looked up, pushing the wet hair out of her eyes. "That is all I get?"

"What else will you have of me? A written apology?"

"Why didn't you tell me before?"

"It's not my usual way of introduction."

"You haven't introduced yourself at all." Robyn deadpanned back. "Why leave me in the dark as to what you are?"

"Are you going to start with all these questions again?"

Robyn slammed her hand on the edge of the tub. "Aye, because you're not telling me anything!"

Gwen's face softened, but her lips were still pressed tightly together. She narrowed her eyes. "Let's go back to that first day. What would you have done waking up in a strange cabin with a strange woman, and then later with a wolf?"

"All right, I guess that would have been too much. But why not tell me later? Why did you always come to me as the wolf and played with me like a friend?"

"Because that was what I wanted, lass," Gwen said. "I wanted you to like me, to see me as a friend and not a bloodthirsty monster. Would you have stayed if you hadn't had the chance to see that the wolf is harmless?"

"If I had left, it wouldn't have been because of the wolf," Robyn answered quietly.

She could see Gwen start at that though she kept her gaze steady. "I might seem harsh to you, but I had no other way to make you see."

"See what?"

"That you can make it on your own. You're no bloody fool, lass. You can think for yourself, and you can make decisions all alone."

"You were mean on purpose?"

"I wasn't mean."

"Well, you made me feel useless and not very welcome."

"Would you have dared to say that to me a few weeks ago?"

Robyn fell silent and smiled inwardly. A few weeks ago her biggest problem had been how to explain to Hunter why she had ran after a wolf to warn it about the Red Riders. Hunter had tried to kill her. Now she was here, talking back to the head of the house and standing her ground and doing it pretty well.

Gwen smiled, really smiled at her, teeth and all. "See, you're contemplating and you're pleased with your answer. Good girl."

"Does that mean I've passed your test?"

"Oh, lass, I haven't even begun testing you." To make it worse, she began to laugh.

Robyn chuckled. “Your good mood is scaring me a little.”

Gwen quirked a brow. “The big wolf you can roughhouse with in the mud and snow, but my happiness worries you?” She rolled her sleeves up and grabbed the water pitcher. “Get your head over that tub and let me wash your hair properly. We wouldn’t want it to be as bad as mine now, would we?”

Robyn only just managed to bow her head before a cascade of cold water hit her.

Chapter 8

A WEEK PASSED WITH HEAVY snowfall keeping the women cabin bound. Gwen went out once or twice to catch something for dinner, but even she was beginning to feel the cold. Sometimes she came home as her wolf though she never let Robyn see her change back. The animal made a bed for itself on the blankets on the floor and let Robyn rest against her furry body. Sometimes Robyn fell asleep on her, but wolf Gwen never seemed to mind.

While Gwen was out hunting for that day's dinner, Robyn brought in several buckets full of water for a bath. Heating it over the fire soon turned the cabin into a steam sauna, but at least it was warm. She soaked in the hot water until her bones melted, then wrapped herself in a towel and waited for Gwen to come home. There were still two buckets gently heating so Gwen could enjoy a hot bath, too.

Robyn sat down and started to brush her hair. She looked around the tiny little cabin and sighed happily. Never in all her life did she think she'd end up in a place like this. She had no husband to cook for and no man to obey. There was nobody she depended on. Except Gwen.

And Gwen had never let Robyn feel like she had to perform like the perfect housewife. She owed Gwen, but she was not owned by her. If she wanted to make Gwen happy, then it was by her own freewill and not her conditioning. And she'd like to give something back for the kindness Gwen had shown her.

"I think I could be happy here," she said to herself. She felt clean and warm. She was safe here, this was home.

The door swung open, and a gush of icy air hit her. She shuddered. It seemed happiness depended a lot on the temperature in the room, and the amount of mud and snow in your entrance! "Gwen, for goodness sake take off those boots and close the door."

Gwen was stomping the snow off her boots. She raised an eyebrow when she saw the steamy room. "Are you trying to open your pores, or did you just feel like using up all our stock of firewood?"

"I've had a bath. And so will you." Robyn stood eye to eye with Gwen, in case it took persuading.

Gwen opened her mouth to speak, but apparently thought twice about it and blinked stupidly at Robyn instead.

"Don't stare at me like a landed fish. Go get your clothes off while I heat the rest of the water."

"The...I..." Robyn felt Gwen's eyes on her as she set about pouring out the hot water. "Lass, aren't you cold wearing only that...that...piece of clothing?"

"It's steaming hot in here; I could easily wear nothing and still stay lovely and warm."

"Nothing?" Gwen shook her head. She made no move to get out of her wet clothes. Her ears were scarlet with the cold, and her hands tainted with faint blood smears. Her hair was a rat's nest of melting snow and mud.

Steam rose from the tub and Robyn reached for the laces of Gwen's vest. Gwen jumped backward.

"What's wrong?" Robyn asked.

"I..."

Impatiently, Robyn pointed at the tub. "It's starting to cool, use it now while I boil some more. Stop behaving like a whelp and get in."

Gwen started to take off her vest.

Robyn placed another towel next to the fire to warm. Then she grabbed a jar from the edge of the tub.

"What's that?" Gwen asked, throwing her dirty clothes in a pile on the floor alongside Robyn's.

"Some herbs I made into a paste," Robyn explained. "This will make your hair smell fresh and help clean your skin."

"Are you politely telling me I smell?"

"I was not raised to speak my thoughts aloud," Robyn said, half-jokingly. "Actually, I was not raised to have thoughts at all."

Robyn lifted the pot of warm water off the fire and turned to the tub. Gwen stood naked before her. Robyn paused. She had never seen such a beautiful female body before.

For all her fuss about taking her clothes off, Gwen did not seem very shy about her nudity now. She stood tall and proud. Her legs were long and lean and perfectly muscled. The flare of her hips tapered up to a tight waist and a flat muscular stomach. She had a body that knew hard work.

And Robyn decided she was excellent at choosing clothes that hid every trace of her femininity.

Robyn smiled involuntarily and felt her cheeks heat as her gaze lingered on Gwen's small round breasts. Without any warning, a vision of her cupping them slid into her mind. What would they feel like? She cleared her throat and shooed the thought away. Gwen stepped into the tub.

"L...let me top up the water," she stammered and watched as Gwen slid her beautiful body into the hot water with a sigh of happiness. "Is it hot enough?"

"Aye, after freezing my ass off out there, anything is warm enough."

"Then I'll wash your hair." Gwen did not try to argue. She dutifully leaned her head back and waited for Robyn to start. Robyn got down on her knees and lifting a pitcher began to pour water over Gwen's head. She took a handful of her herb paste and massaged it into Gwen's scalp. Her breathing hitched, and Robyn felt the tension leave her body almost instantly.

"That's nice, lass. And it smells good."

"I wanted to thank you for your kindness and, well, for teaching me to listen to myself," Robyn said. "So thank you."

"You're welcome, and thanks for the bath and all."

Robyn kept massaging her head until Gwen began to doze off. Quietly, she tip-toed over to the stack of fresh clothes she kept next to her bed. She pulled a shirt over her head and grabbed the pants she had been busy sewing for the last few days while Gwen was out and about. The stupidity of heavy skirts when wading through the snow or struggling through the undergrowth had finally galvanized her into action. She needed something that closed around her ankles, something that let her lift her legs and stride out. With skillful hands, she had redesigned her old skirt into trousers. She was proud at being so practical and brave. So much had changed for her in these few weeks. No, she had changed so much for herself.

She pulled her hair up with a leather band and went over to the stove to retrieve the next pot of heated water. As it poured into the tub Gwen woke up.

"Ouch, that's hot," she complained before her eyes fell on Robyn's new attire. "And so are you."

Robyn felt her cheeks burn but smiled proudly nevertheless.

"You've a fine ass for trousers." Gwen reached out to grab a wet handful.

"What's gotten into you?" Robyn asked, neatly side-stepping. She was not entirely sure if she should feel offended or flattered. She did feel excited, though.

Gwen couldn't hide her smile. "I'm sorry. I'm clean, I'm warm, and I'm happy, and the wolf wants to play. I should get out." She rose from the tub, cascading water and towered over Robyn like some mythic goddess.

"Ah. The wolf. That's my cue," Robyn said and pushed the sleeves of her shirt up. "Change, please."

"What?"

"Is your fur washed clean?"

"My fur?"

"Yes, is the wolf as clean as you are?"

"Well, um—"

"All right then, change."

"It's not that easy."

"Why not?" Robyn asked. "Do you need to be angry to change? Shall I poke you with a stick?"

"It's... I don't do it in front of people. It's a private, intimate thing."

"You realize you're telling me this while you're standing dripping wet and buck naked in front of me?"

Gwen grabbed for the towel. "The wolf is clean, believe me, I took care of that," she said, as she wrapped the towel around herself.

Unhappy, but respecting her wishes, Robyn stepped back to let her out step of the tub. "I'm sorry, I didn't—"

"It's all right, lass. I thank you for the bath." Gwen roughly toweled her hair dry.

"Have you thought about maybe brushing it, just this once?"

Gwen stopped and peeped out from under the towel. "Brush?"

"Yes, you know, like combing it through with your fingers, only more efficient. It might help against the felting."

"Are you trying to make a fine lady out of me?" Gwen asked in a light voice and with a sparkle in her eyes.

"We already established you'd rather be the gentleman," Robyn grinned. "I'm just pragmatic."

"Like with the trousers?"

"Absolutely."

Gwen put on some clean clothes before sitting on the bed to let Robyn brush her short hair. "Feeling better now?" Gwen asked after they were done.

"Yes, I am. And so should you. You should be saying, 'Thank you, Robyn, for making me look clean and decent for once in a lifetime.' That's what you should be saying."

Gwen turned to look at her, her eyes huge and broke into a hearty laugh. Robyn wanted to be offended, but it was so good to hear Gwen's laugh she just couldn't.

"All right," Gwen said, catching her breath. "Thank you, lass, for cleaning the crusty old wolf up."

The happiness in Gwen's words was overshadowed by one small thing. "You know, I have a name, too," Robyn said. "I'm not just lass." Hunter had called her by every interchangeable pet name but her own.

Gwen's eyes grew serious, the sparkle fizzled out. She took Robyn's hand. "I know that, Robyn. But you're the only lass I'll ever have, so no chance mixing that up."

Robyn regarded her for a second. They were sitting so close she felt the heat radiate from Gwen's body.

"The tub," Gwen said and leaped to her feet "Let's pour it behind the cabin, so we don't break our necks on ice come the morning."

"What?" Robyn was perplexed by the sudden change of subject. "We can't lift a tub full of water."

"Of course we can." Gwen already had the tub by the handles while Robyn debated how lunatic the endeavor was. "Come on and at least try."

Robyn sighed and shook her head. She wasn't certain what had happened in the past week. Gwen had become a friendly, good-natured person once Robyn had found out she was the wolf. And the fluttering in Robyn's gut that she had first thought was relief at escaping her fate as a village girl, was becoming something she'd never felt before.

"How do we do this?" she asked.

"Open the door, and then we'll lift it and carry it outside."

She gave Gwen a look that hopefully translated as something like 'are you crazy?', and opened the door anyway.

"Now, one, two, three...lift."

To Robyn's surprise, Gwen lifted the tub off the floor on her own with a mighty grunt. Her enthusiasm for the task was evident. It was a challenge or a game to her, Robyn was unsure which. She moved backward through the door guiding Gwen's every step out onto the slippery porch. "Be aware of the—" Gwen tripped over her own feet and fell over. Robyn tried to grab at the tub as it slipped out of her grasp. She pulled it to the side, so the water poured out all over the porch steps, exactly where they didn't want it.

Gwen lay spread-eagle in the snow.

"Are you hurt?" Robyn knelt beside her, muddying her pants.

"So much for pouring it behind the cabin to save us from slipping." Gwen pushed herself up onto her elbows and looked over to where the tub lay. "This makes us even, I suppose."

Robyn followed her gaze. "What do you mean?" A snowball smacked her on the side of the head.

Gwen laughed. "I owe you that from yesterday."

"Oh? Well, that pretty fur of yours isn't so white when I do this." Robyn threw a snowball of her own.

Gwen ducked. "Not today, you don't. You made a mess of me at the lake yesterday. Now I'm nice and clean!" Another snowball whizzed past her ear. Gwen leaped to her feet running back a few steps, laughing. "Look at you, lass. Hitting back, and ordering me around in my own cabin just because you're wearing trousers now."

Robyn hesitated for a second and thought about that. She had become more confident, and she was learning to trust her judgment. All that she owed to Gwen. "You've done so much for me," she said.

Gwen's scoffing smile fell away, and she stood watching Robyn intently.

Robyn threw her snowball and caught her bang in the middle of the chest, then ran away shrieking with laughter with Gwen hard on her heels. Gwen grabbed her, and they both tumbled onto the snow. Robyn fell on top of her, and they lay nose to nose.

"Got you," Gwen said quietly, her gaze fixed on Robyn's.

"Maybe I've got you," Robyn's voice was barely a whisper. She could feel the heat from Gwen's body, despite the coldness of the day.

"I could kiss you right here and now in the snow," Gwen said. "But you wouldn't want that, would you? That would be bad for a village girl." A gleam of something else, something hard and burning entered her eyes.

"Who said I'm a village girl?"

Gwen gave a short, hard laugh. "All the beliefs and values pummeled into you since birth say so."

"And what did that get me? A man who hunts creatures that have never done him any harm? A man who made me an outcast for disobeying him, and will probably marry the next woman who comes along if she is stupid enough and keeps her mouth shut. Oh, and let's not forget my grandmother who happily threw me into his arms. I'll bet she never once questioned what happened to me. She'd rather believe every vile word out of Hunter's mouth. She'd prefer me to be dead than to have lost such a catch as the wonderful Captain Wolfmounter."

"Wolfmounter led you to me." Gwen pointed out. Her hands slid down Robyn's back spreading a delicious heat. Robyn shivered, amazed at how easy they were together. How well their bodies seemed to fit.

"I want you to kiss me," Robyn said. She was falling forward, pressing their foreheads together. "Right here. In the snow."

If this had been a fairy tale they would have kissed. And in the dying rays of the sunset Robyn's hair would glow in the pale light, and Gwen's strong arms would wrap around her, pressing her close. But it wasn't a fairy tale. Instead, they went back to the cabin where, for the first time, Gwen chose the comfortable bed over her usual pile of blankets.

Chapter 9

WHITNEY WOLFMOUNTER AWOKE TO THE tweeting of the nesting birds outside her window, much as she had every morning since spring had arrived. She had been Mrs. Hunter Wolfmounter for four months, and she was the proudest woman in the village. Her hand drifted to the small swell of her belly. She had become pregnant very quickly, perhaps even on their wedding night, and it made her unutterably proud. She sat on the edge of the bed and rubbed her bulge with oil-slick fingers. She hoped to have no stretch marks so Hunter would still find her body attractive after their son was born. A soft knock at the door shook her from her daydreams as Rose entered.

"Good morning, sister. Did you sleep well?" Rose asked.

Whitney inclined her head like the mistress of the house should, and sat down at her vanity table. Rose stood behind her and started combing her hair.

"Hunter loves how my curls fall around my face." Whitney examined herself in the mirror.

"Yes, you're a rare beauty," Rose said, mechanically.

"Will Hunter be home for dinner tonight?"

Rose put the brush aside and started to plait the hair into a fine knot. "He has business with his men again, but he said he'd go to the market with us tomorrow."

"Oh, well, he is the captain." Whitney sighed. "He has important Red Rider things to take care of." She tried to appear gracious and understanding. She didn't want Rose to know that, deep down, she was worried. Since she'd found out she was pregnant, Hunter hadn't shared their bed for anything other than sleeping. It was as if he didn't desire her anymore. "I knew what lay ahead of me when I married a man of such standing in the community."

Rose set out her clothes for the day. "He has all the standing a man like him can handle," she mumbled. "But he always comes running back to his loving wife with his sword pressed tightly to his leg."

"But he hasn't a sword," Whitney corrected her. "Only his bow and a dagger. Though I appreciate you trying to comfort me."

Rose gave a snort that turned into a soft cough.

"You're not coming down with a cold, are you?" Whitney flung a protective hand over her belly.

"No." Rose soothed her. "Something caught in my throat."

Whitney looked at the dress Rose had laid out for her. "I should wear the pink today."

"No, the brown dress is best for cooking in." Rose held it up for her to examine. It wasn't the most beautiful, but Whitney knew she wouldn't look awful in it either.

"All right then, I suppose it will do."

Rose helped her into it, then fastened the laces on the back. "Greta and Granny will be here in about an hour.

That gives you enough time for breakfast." Rose made the bed. "I've prepared everything for you downstairs."

"I do appreciate your kindness." Whitney patted her sister on the back. Rose flinched and drew away. Whitney was torn between regret for her sister and pride in her husband.

"Rose," she said softly. "If a man cares about you he will take pains to make sure your education is correct. Even if he has to exhaust himself beating you."

Rose looked away. Whitney presumed she was too embarrassed at the attention Hunter was showing her. But there was no need for that. Whitney was so proud of her sister! Rose had finally submitted to her female inclinations and become a wonderful house help.

"Hunter's been so kind in allowing you time to adjust," Whitney continued. "And you're making such good progress in learning your place around a man. It makes me so happy to see that you've finally grown into a fine woman who will be a joy for some lucky village man to marry."

Rose's face blazed. She bustled around the bedroom tidying, her gaze averted from her sister. Whitney smiled. Now she had further embarrassed Rose with her talk of a husband.

"Let's go down for breakfast," she said, awkwardly changing the subject.

When they were on the stairs, she gently tried to bring up the topic again. "We may even find a nice man for you tomorrow at the spring feast," she said but refrained from touching Rose's shoulder again.

"Maybe I will find myself a nice ax, too."

The vehemence of Rose's answer startled Whitney. "Why? Do we need more wood for the oven?" she asked uncertainly. She didn't want her household to look mismanaged when her visitors came. "Heaven knows what portions Granny will want to cook."

"I've taken care of the wood," Rose assured her.

Whitney sat down heavily at the kitchen table and smoothed her hand over belly again. The boy she was carrying would be strong, like his father. "Granny's visit has got me thinking."

"Don't hurt yourself," Rose said and slid a cup of hot water away from her elbow as if to underscore her warning.

"Thank you for looking after me so well." Whitney grabbed her hand and squeezed it. "I know you were friends with Robyn and you miss her. And it pains me to see how Hunter is still agonizing over how he couldn't save her. It was a terrible loss, but he's sworn to avenge her."

"Oh, I smell his anguish every night when he comes home," Rose muttered. Whitney agreed. Some nights he came home so wrapped in his grief that he could hardly speak for slurring.

"But there has to be the sunshine after the rain," she said with a smile. "Hunter chose me to lessen his pain, and he was so lucky to get a sister as well. And look at us now! Father couldn't be happier. He has one of his girls married to a fine gentleman, and his other daughter will soon be ready to follow suit. We should thank Robyn for the great service she rendered. Do you think we should light church candles in her memory for a week, or would that be too much?"

Rose teared up. Whitney was surprised at Rose being so emotional about her idea. It was only candles, after all. Then, Rose was on her feet. "I changed my mind," she said. "We do need more wood." And she almost ran for the back door.

"Are you going to chop some more?" Whitney called after her in surprise. "Right now?" She still hadn't been served breakfast.

"Definitely!" Rose called back, before heading for the garden and grabbing the heavy ax. Through the window, Whitney could see her splitting the logs with great enthusiasm. Whitney was happy to see her sister so at ease with herself. Rose was becoming a fine, upstanding woman, at last.

"Come on, lass, it really isn't that hard."

"I told you I couldn't do it."

"But you'll probably have to one day."

"Why would I?"

"Well, if you go back to the village maybe." Gwen shrugged.

"I won't go back there."

After the frost had left their little clearing, nature started to regain her strength. The grass became greener, and beautiful birds sang of new blossoms and the warming sun. Gwen had taken advantage of a sunny morning to take Robyn out to practice self-defense and hand-to-hand fighting. Robyn didn't see the point; she was unlikely to be attacked out here. And if danger did come near then she could hide, for surely her fantastic hearing would let her know when anyone was close by. But Gwen insisted she should at least learn how to throw a punch…just in case.

Robyn refused to hit her, though.

"Robyn, darling, if you can't hit me, what will you do when someone else comes at you?"

"Like who?"

Gwen rolled her eyes. "Anybody who comes along."

"But we haven't seen a single soul for months."

"First of all, it was winter and all the forest paths were knee deep in snow." A smile tugged at the corner of Gwen's mouth. "And secondly, you wouldn't have been able to see much with your head stuck under the covers."

Robyn blushed. "Are you accusing me of being inattentive?"

"In bed or out here?" Gwen shot back smoothly.

Laughing indignantly, Robyn rolled up her sleeves. "All right then, where shall I punch you?"

"Right here," Gwen said, lifting her arms and showing her bare hands.

Robyn made a fist and smacked it into Gwen's palm.

"That was less than weak." Gwen was amused. "Again."

Robyn tried harder. Gwen didn't flinch.

"Again. Harder."

Her next punch came faster, but without much result. "I'm no good at this," she said, frustrated.

Gwen agreed. "No, you're not. Now try again."

"But what for?" Robyn asked. Her shoulders slumped.

"Because I said so!"

Gwen's sudden bark made her cringe in reflex at the shouted words. Embarrassed, she gathered herself together and straightened her spine. "Don't yell at me!"

"You seem incapable of doing anything right without being yelled at." Gwen's tone was low.

Robyn narrowed her eyes and answered in the same low tone, "Don't speak to me like that, Gwen, I mean it. It's threatening."

"You're mixing up threats with truths." Gwen towered over her. "If a man passed by and ordered you to, I bet you'd be on your knees to serve him in the blink of an eye."

That was a lie, as well as being outright mean. Robyn felt her anger boil. Gwen had no right to speak that way. "I won't let you talk to me like that!"

"You won't? Let's suppose I abandoned you right here in the woods. Just turned around and walked away. How long would you survive with your fancy village skills?" Gwen laughed and turned to go. Something hot and furious broke loose inside Robyn. She ran at Gwen and pushed her as hard as she could. Gwen flew through the air like a rag doll and slammed into a nearby tree.

Robyn stood rooted to the spot in shock. It was only when Gwen opened her eyes and rubbed the back of her head that Robyn's legs began to move. She ran to her and knelt beside her.

"Gwen, are you all right?" she cried. "I'm so sorry, I—"

"I'm fine." Gwen soothed her, taking her hand. "That was exactly what I wanted you to do."

"Are you insane? I could have killed you!" Robyn's voice rose.

Gwen grinned at her. "Of course you could have, and that's what will make me a lot less worried when you're alone out here in the woods."

Robyn eyed her skeptically. Then she decided to let it go, because Gwen, as usual, had got what she wanted. She leaned forward for a kiss and was immediately pulled into warm arms and held against a strong beating heart.

"You know I didn't mean what I said earlier."

"But it could have been true not that long ago." Robyn sighed.

"You seemed sure about not going back to the village. Why?"

Smoothing her hand down Gwen's belly, Robyn shrugged. "There isn't anything there for me." They lay together in silence, listening to the birds and the wind hissing through the fir trees all around them.

Finally, Gwen struggled to her feet. She held out her hand. "Come, lass," she said. "Let's eat."

After lunch, Gwen scrubbed the dishes while Robyn wiped down the table. Their conversation kept racing around her mind, that there was nothing in the village for her. What she had said to Gwen was true, there was no one else she cared about in the way she cared for Gwen, her stubborn, blonde-haired giant of a woman. But there were still some friends she missed.

"...carrots tomorrow?"

Snapping out of her thoughts, Robyn turned around. "Huh?"

"Shall we sow the carrot seeds tomorrow? The earth is warm enough." Gwen's expression turned to concern.

"Still thinking about the push?" she asked. "I told you it was nothing."

"I was thinking about what you said about being safe." It had not entered her mind once the whole of winter because she had felt safe then, and still did. But Gwen's insistence on her learning to fight now had her questioning how much protection they needed from the villagers, or anything else that happened along. Was her new home really under threat from her old life out here?

"You are safe with me," Gwen insisted.

"And what about you?"

"Haven't you just proved yourself worthy of being my protector?" Gwen laughed, rubbing her stomach. She grew serious though when Robyn didn't join in. "These woods are only dangerous for those who do not know them."

"Like the Sweets." A picture of the strange siblings appearing in the village came to her mind.

"What?"

Robyn looked up. "A friend of mine and her brother survived an entire winter in these woods." A strange look flashed over Gwen's face, but she said nothing, so Robyn continued. "They were traveling from village to village after the terrible harvests all those years ago when they lost their parents. They roamed the forest all winter and in spring found their way to our village. No one knows how they survived. They haven't shared that story with anyone, not even their friends. The villagers assume Hans looked after them both, protecting his sister as a good brother should." She shrugged, somehow that explanation didn't work anymore. "Anyway, I'm glad it was you who found me and not some dangerous beast."

"There're lots of traitorous beasts in these woods," Gwen said and reached out for her. "That's why you need to protect yourself…from all of them."

When her grip grew so tight it hurt, Robyn put her hand on top of the warm fingers and squeezed gently. "I'll be all right as long as we're together." But there was still something seething inside Gwen. Robyn felt it in her guts. Was she really afraid something could happen to them? Was that why she had been so eager to train Robyn in self-defense? Whatever it was, Robyn had no chance to ask, for Gwen pulled off her vest and shirt and was now striding toward the door.

"I need to…be outside", she said through gritted teeth.

Robyn nodded. Gwen never wanted company when she turned into the wolf. Going by her recent behavior, she'd be gone a while, and Robyn knew better than to asked her where she'd go. Gwen would come back when she was ready, and that was that.

"Take care," she said and Gwen smiled at her before she went outside.

When the door closed, Robyn leaned against the backrest of her chair and thought about their safety. Was there an imminent threat? Spring had arrived, so the Riders would start patrolling the forest edges soon. Hunter had probably married someone else once she was out of the picture, so would he still be after the wolf? Would he still be after her? She wondered how far the cabin was from the village, and would she and Gwen be safe here, despite what Gwen said? The curiosity inside her was getting the better of her; she wanted to know what had happened during her absence. What lies had Hunter spread about her disappearance? Had he blamed her for the wolf escaping? And even though she might be safe here in the woods, what had become of her friends?

The houses on the edge of the village were empty. At first she was confused as to why, but as she sneaked further in, she became aware of the date. It was the spring feast day. From a back street, she peered into the market square, her enhanced eyesight allowing her to focus in on a hundred little details, like Goldie selling linen and gemstones from her stall. Her husband, Spindlefinger was behind the counter of his wine booth. The whole square was full of people, and the Red Riders were scattered through the crowd supposedly keeping the peace.

Robyn hunkered down behind a wall and watched the people she had known for years going about their business. She was fascinated by how familiar it all was. The faces of friends and neighbors, the sights and scents of her village. Once upon a time, it had been the only home she had ever known. She saw little Ebony running after her brothers, carrying armloads of shopping and looking exhausted. Ebony never complained; on the contrary, she saw it as her duty to take care of her menfolk. Right behind her came Ash with a basket full of groceries. She too was a good girl, waiting for the day her father found her a husband and hoping that, unlike her father, he would be a good, kind man.

Robyn suppressed a shiver. It was not only Ebony and Ash; it was all of the young women. All of her friends, since they had been little girls, had been in thrall to the village men. Men made rules and the women obeyed. It made them happy. It really did. Her throat closed over. She too had thought she was happy, but then she had never known a different life.

It was time to go. She was about to leave when the great Hunter Wolfmounter strolled into the market like he owned the place. On his arm, he paraded what could only be his beautiful new wife. Robyn nearly choked on her spit. Whitney Prospector? Had he married Whitney? Why on earth had he married one of the most stupid girls in the village? And had she a swollen belly? She didn't know whether to laugh or scream at the surreal picture. Eventually, a laugh bubbled in her throat. On second thought, Whitney was the best match for him; she was eager to serve, had a shallow personality, but was beautiful enough to look good on his arm. She'd give him many handsome sons, who would no doubt grow up to be just as charming as their father.

Robyn was satisfied she had seen enough. Hunter had got what he wanted. He would keep playing the fearless captain and rule over the Riders, the village, and his wife, and good luck to them all.

A huddled figure following a few steps behind the Wolfmounters caught her attention. With a gasp, Robyn recognized Rose. The insolent and prickly Rose Prospector trundled along behind her sister and her husband. But this Rose was hunched under a load of shopping. She seemed shrunken and small compared to the big frame of her brother-in-law. She barely looked up from under her hood. Hunter didn't take any notice of her other than piling more shopping onto her already large load. Rose sank under the extra weight but didn't utter a word. Robyn felt sick. She wanted to rip the macabre scene to pieces. It was all wrong. It was a lie!

Two guards turned into the side alley where she was hiding. Despite all her anger, she couldn't risk being seen. On silent feet, she crept back the way she had come and vanished back into the dark forest.

Robyn ran along the earthen paths between the trees. Here the air was cooler and the shadows longer. Especially the shadow coming up behind her. She slowed down and squeezed through a gap into a quiet copse. The shadow had gone, but the sound of boots slipping over mossy stones was audible to her ears. Then came the smell of a familiar human being. She knew who was behind her, what she didn't know was whether to relax or stay alert. Gwen had told her that to attack was better than to run, so she pressed her hands into fists and spun around with a sharp cry.

Rose jumped backward in shock.

"Why on earth did you do that? You scared me!" She fumed, once she regained her composure.

"I wanted to," Robyn said. "Until I know whether you're friend or foe?"

Rose put her hands on her hips. "When was I not your friend?"

"Maybe when you became Hunter's personal assistant."

Rose flushed violently. "What else could I do after you left me? Why didn't you tell me you were going?"

Robyn's gut clenched. "Things happened so fast, there was no time."

"You could have come to me that night, but instead you chose the woods." Rose's voice was quiet.

"I didn't choose; it was my only option."

They regarded each other in silence, and it occurred to Robyn that neither of them was panting though Rose must have run even faster than she had to catch up with her.

"At first I thought you were another vision," Rose spoke at last. "I had a few of those the first weeks after you'd gone. But this time you seemed so real. And then I thought to hell with it! I gave Whitney some silly excuse and sneaked away after you without anybody noticing."

"Are you sure nobody saw you?" Robyn asked with a rush of panic. Rose smiled and calmed her down.

"I'm sure," she said. "And I'm so glad I didn't imagine you." A lightness crept into her voice.

Robyn's head whirled. She could barely make sense of Rose's words. "Oh, Rose." She closed the gap between them. "I'm so glad you haven't changed though I feared the worst when I saw you at the market."

"I only play pretend and wait my chance." Rose pulled her into a hug. "But I hope you have finally changed, my friend."

Robyn pressed her face into the crook of Rose's neck. "Oh, I have. And you wouldn't believe how much."

"Greta and I were convinced you weren't dead, but there was no way to prove it and expose that bastard," Rose said.

"Wait, what do you mean, I'm not dead?" Robyn pulled back.

Rose raised her eyebrows. "I don't know what happened in the woods, but I sure as hell don't believe that Wolfmounter was too late to save you. Or that his heart broke in two when the wolf dragged you off." She mocked a sad face.

Robyn's mouth hung open. "The fucktard!"

Rose covered her mouth and giggled. "Oh, milady, what a word. Did you learn that in the woods?"

"And still too good for him." Robyn spat. "I was in the woods when an arrow flew past me. It missed me by inches, Rose. I looked around, thinking that maybe some hunters hadn't seen me. Hunter stood behind me, and he was aiming right at me," she said bitterly. "I believe if Hans hadn't come along he would have killed me there and then."

"So you ran for your life." Rose was awestruck.

"Yes, I ran. At that moment I honestly believed I had done something incredibly evil. I had put the life of a wild wolf before the safety of the village. I believed he was right to be so angry with me."

Rose shook her head; her knuckles were white with fury. "I knew it!" She looked at Robyn, her eyes hot but gentle. "But now you see what a bastard he is, don't you?"

"I do," Robyn smiled. "But all those women." She nodded in the direction of the village. "They don't."

Rose nodded sadly. "And for some of them, all hope is lost."

"Your sister?"

They both chuckled. "They make a lovely pair, don't they?"

Rose looked away, and Robyn asked in a tight voice. "What happened after I left?"

"Oh, after Hunter married my sister, to avoid losing his money on your canceled wedding, by the way. He saw it as his duty as my brother-in-law to make me a suitable wife for one of his Riders."

"So, he tried to tame you?"

"And he is so successful at it. Didn't you see how good I was at the market earlier?"

"I saw a perfectly behaved young village woman going about her duties."

Rose smoothed her hands down her skirt and tried to smile brightly. "I have to keep myself together. But Hunter truly believes that he's won."

"So why are you still there?" Robyn asked. "Why didn't you run away a long time ago? You were always against the way the village women were treated."

"You saw how our women behave. Doesn't their stupidity pain you as much as it does me?" Rose asked.

Robyn nodded in agreement. She wasn't sure how to explain it to Rose. "I don't know how it happened, but these last few months living in the forest have opened my eyes."

"I understand exactly."

"You do?"

"You should thank me," Rose said, her eyes sparkled with excitement. "Do you remember who sent you to the forest for herbs?"

"Are you saying…?" Did Rose set her up? Impossible!

"I did it on purpose," Rose confessed and put her hand up to silence Robyn before she interrupted. "Please don't be angry with me, Robyn. I've beaten myself up a million times over it. But in the end things turned out for the better, didn't they?"

Robyn locked her arms across her chest. "You sent me to the forest when you knew a wolf was out there." It was a statement, not a question.

Rose averted her gaze. "Let me tell you a fairy tale, all right?" She looked for permission. Robyn nodded for her to go on.

"Once upon a time an orphaned brother and sister had to survive in the woods on their own. The boy fell unconscious from hunger, and the girl, despite her fever, went to search for berries. A raven haired, beautiful woman, clad all in dark leather crossed the girl's path. She took pity on her and gave her food and drink. Her only request was that the girl should never tell her brother about the mysterious woman who'd saved them. It was a promise the girl kept because it gave her the opportunity to see the dark woman over and over again. Time passed, and the siblings survived the winter into spring. The boy never knew anyone else lived in the woods besides him and his sister. And the girl? She became friends with the dark woman and her fair haired female companion. The woman saw potential in the girl and together with her friend she chose to give her the gift of sight."

Robyn had sat down on a fallen tree trunk. A chill was building in her body. The story was unnerving her.

"It soon became time for the siblings to move on," Rose continued. "The girl promised to come back and visit the women in the woods. The boy and girl found shelter in a small village at the edge of the forest and the girl kept her promise. Every time she came back she told her friend about the women of the village, and how with her own gift of sight she could see their blindness to the way their men treated them. She wanted all those women to see the truth just as she could, and her friend decided to help her."

Robyn's lungs nearly burst with the breath she was holding. "And so the Black Wolf came to the village," she whispered. Rose nodded, her eyes teary.

The Black Wolf. Gwen's lost love, her other half. Robyn shivered. Gwen had never talked about another person living in the woods with her though Robyn had always known there must have been somebody once. And losing that somebody had made Gwen hate the village. Robyn saw it all now, and it explained Gwen's reaction to her story about the Sweets. She looked at Rose in disbelief. "It was Greta who let the Black Wolf into the village. It had to bite all women so they could see."

"But she only managed to bite me before Hunter chased her to her grave," Rose said.

If the wolf hadn't come, then Hunter wouldn't have killed her, and Gwen would still be in love with the beautiful, dark haired woman from the woods. Robyn bit her tongue; was it wrong to be relieved that that someone who once owned Gwen's heart was no threat anymore? Robyn's gut clenched. It was wrong to think such mean thoughts. It was the greatest loss Robyn could ever imagine. And to think that maybe Gwen had not always been this stubborn, sarcastic hermit in the woods but a cheerful and loving woman? It made her heart ache. No, Robyn called her thoughts to order. The Black Wolf was a dark figure from the past, Gwen and Robyn were here and now, they were the present.

"Greta was devastated. Her friend had been killed, and she lost heart. She didn't want to risk helping the women again. As for me, I had been bitten. I couldn't stop thinking about how it could be."

"So you lured me into the woods as part of your plan," Robyn said. "How did you know the white wolf would be there? And that it would just bite me and not kill me?"

Rose's cheeks blazed. "It was wrong of me. I'm sorry. I knew if Whitney overheard me send you into the forest she wouldn't hesitate to tell Hunter. I was certain he would play the knight in shining armor and run after you. The wolf would smell him from miles away."

"You've lost me." Robyn struggled to follow this part of Rose's story.

With a snort, Rose continued, "I hoped the wolf would kill Hunter, then, seeing your resemblance to the dark woman—"

"You thought she'd bite me because she found me hot?" Robyn interrupted angrily. Rose's plan was preposterous.

Rose tried to soothe her. "I didn't have any other plan. You were my first choice. You were always the brainy one out of all my friends."

Robyn rubbed her hands over her cold face and sighed. "At least that part of the plan worked."

With a small, sad laugh, Rose said: "I was always the hot-headed one. I'm not known for thinking things through."

"But you managed to keep your cool living with Hunter."

"I didn't at first. He beat me pretty bad. He knew I didn't believe his story about what happened to you. I told him you'd come back and expose him. I believed that so strongly." She sighed. "But winter came and still you didn't return. I had expected you would come to me after you found out what the wolf bite meant." Her voice was full of quiet defeat.

Robyn felt sick seeing how her friend's hopes had been crushed. "Rose, I didn't know to go to you," she explained, and gently squeezed her shoulder. "But I did find someone who taught me how to think for myself."

Rose pulled away, her eyes wide, her smile dirty. "So she did find you hot!"

"Pardon me?"

"Well, Greta had told me it could happen," Rose was talking too fast and Robyn struggled to understand what she was so excited about. "But she swore it wouldn't go that far."

"What are you talking about?"

She slowed down and at least had the decency to blush. "The wolf's bite gives you the power to see. For most of us that means we start to think about our situation and learn to question our lives, and some of us can even find the true nature of their hearts."

Robyn was stunned.

"You are happy, aren't you?" Rose asked.

"Very happy."

"And wouldn't you want that for all of them?"

Robyn hesitated. "The village women?"

Nodding with great enthusiasm, Rose said, "Maybe we could repeat the night of the Black Wolf."

Taking a step back, Robyn shook her head vehemently. "No, not after what happened to her."

"But we could make it different!" Rose insisted. Her eyes flashed. "I could take a knife and stab him to death—"

"Rose!"

But she wouldn't stop. "I want to help them and I can't do it alone. Greta is too afraid after that last time, so I thought you could help me. That was why I chose you in the first place. But you left, and I had to start all over again. I'm tired, Robyn. I can't keep pretending for much longer, the struggle is too hard for one girl on her own. And I am all alone."

"Shush," Robyn soothed, wiping at Rose's tears. Rose didn't seem to notice. "You're not alone, Rose. You could come with me."

"And the others? What about them? No, I will find a way. That bastard Wolfmounter will not win. He might have broken Greta and scared you away, but he won't get to me, I—"

"All right!" Robyn stopped the angry ramble. "Tell me what your plan is and I might find a way to help."

Chapter 10

It was almost dark when Robyn arrived back at the cabin. She worried about Rose's absence from the village, but the girl was clever, and her excuses would be good.

They had worked out a plan that might work, but Robyn wasn't sure if she could risk her newfound life and love for it. Rose had understood this and made her a final offer. She would wait at their meeting place two days from now, and if Robyn didn't come, she'd know that help wasn't to be expected from the women of the woods.

Robyn's thoughts were a jumble. Not only because of their risky plan, but now she knew about Gwen's past as well. So many questions were whirling in her head; she had no idea where to start.

The decision was made for her, though. The cabin door burst open so hard it hit the wall and broke the handle.

Gwen strode towards her; an angry red flush creeping up her neck. "Where the fuck have you been?"

Startled by her tone more than the anger on her face, Robyn stopped dead in her tracks. "I was at the village," she said, quietly.

A vein at Gwen's temple throbbed. Robyn couldn't quite read the look Gwen threw at her then. "You said you wouldn't go back." She sounded taken aback.

"I know," Robyn hurried to explain. "I hadn't planned on it at first, but I…I had a feeling that I might be needed."

"Needed?"

"And I was right," she continued. "I met my friend Rose. Hunter married her sister, Whitney Prospector, so he's her brother-in-law now, and he beats her. She needs help. I should have been there for her, but I wasn't. I was with you. And I'm so glad for that, but still, I should have been—" The touch of Gwen's cold fingers on her cheek stopped her short.

"I didn't understand a word of that, lass." Her voice was soft and urgent. "But I never want to come home and find you missing ever again. Are we clear on that?"

Robyn wanted to tell Gwen that she was no puppy to be ordered around, when instead she stood on her tiptoes, and kissed the woman she had come to love on the lips.

"All right," she said, simply. "But let me tell you what happened, please, because it's important."

Gwen nodded and let go of her. "Let's go inside."

As expected the door wouldn't close now, but they could fix that later. Gwen sat down at the table while Robyn moved about the cabin, too fidgety to sit. "I sneaked back into the village to try and find Rose," she said and began her story.

"Who is this Rose?" Gwen asked, leaning forward.

"She is a close friend," Robyn explained excitedly, her words coming faster and faster. "In fact, our very first meeting was by courtesy of Rose. She sent me into the forest to search for herbs. And now Hunter, my betrothed, or rather my ex-betrothed, has married Rose's sister. He was there. In the market. I saw him. I can't believe he married so soon after I was gone!" She snorted scornfully. "Anyway, the real problem is Rose. Hunter has total authority over her because he married Whitney."

"Of course he has. You told me this already," Gwen said, barely able to stop rolling her eyes.

"But that's just it!" Robyn sat down beside Gwen and fixed her with an avid stare. "All these village women think that's the way of it. To be second class and serve the menfolk." She grew agitated again. "Even I was of that opinion once, but you helped me see through it. And with your help, all of them could have their eyes opened. Please, Gwen, no woman should have to live like that."

Gwen looked back at her blankly, and Robyn wasn't sure she'd been precise enough about what the women had to endure, with what the women did voluntarily. "Listen, I—"

"No!" Gwen's voice was like ice. "Nothing could ever get me to help any of them."

Robyn knew then she had been too precipitous. She struggled with herself but decided to speak up, to maybe get Gwen to listen. "I know what happened the first time."

Gwen winced and wouldn't look at Robyn.

"You and the Black Wolf wanted to help Greta. The wolf never threatened the village, she just wanted to enable these women to see for themselves. But Hunter prevented it."

Gwen crossed her arms and stared at the table.

Robyn continued. "Rose and I have a plan that leaves Hunter out of the picture. He won't be there to ruin it this time." Her voice turned softer. "I can't imagine how much it must have hurt to lose her, but don't you want to finish the task your mate started?"

Gwen stared at her, her eyes cold. "There is only one task I need to finish." She spoke in a dire voice. "I have nothing to do with the village. I take care of myself. Nobody else is my business. I don't need to help those people."

"But you helped me?" Robyn was confused. "You showed mercy from that first day when you refused to kill neither Hunter nor me."

Gwen averted her eyes. "I only spared you because I didn't want you to see me rip that murderer into pieces. I could smell him," she spat out. "I always hoped to get him alone in my woods some day, but he was too afraid. He can only kill the coward's way. He never entered the forest alone until the day he followed you."

"He wanted to protect me from the evil in the forest."

Gwen let out a dark laugh. "Aye, because he thought it would be safe so close to the village, and he could play the hero again. I wanted to rip him open."

Gwen's hands were flat on the table now, and her nails were digging into the soft wood. Robyn watched fascinated, but Gwen didn't seem to notice the pain.

"But you didn't because of me," Robyn whispered. "You wanted to protect me."

"No." Gwen stared down at her bloodied nails. "I didn't want to kill an innocent and set others on my track."

"But even if you had killed only him they would have found his body."

Her smile was cruel. "They wouldn't."

Robyn stood. "So you bit me...for what?" She was afraid of the answer but willed herself not to back away.

"Maybe to make you see the rat inside the shining armor?" Gwen shrugged. "I don't know. Maybe I wanted to make sure you wouldn't storm after me and kill me to impress your young stallion."

"Stop talking as if I worshiped the ground he walks on," Robyn said, but less forcefully.

"But isn't that how it's supposed to be down in your little village?"

Robyn wanted to deny this but found she couldn't, so she tried the different approach. "You say you don't know why you bit me," she said. "So why were you lurking under my window? You were calling to me to follow you."

Gwen shook her head. "I wasn't there for you. I thought that maybe the dutiful captain would stop by to check on his sick girl, and I could grab him on the way."

"That is not true!" Robyn said. "There were many opportunities to grab him if you had wanted to. And if your grudge against him is as deep as you try and make out, then it wouldn't have mattered if I was with him that day or not. You would have killed us both in a blind rage. Instead, you opted for biting me, for opening my eyes."

"Maybe I shouldn't have," Gwen said.

Despite the verbal slap, Robyn managed to stand her ground. "And what about these months here with you? You've taught me self-worth and self-respect. You wanted to help me, and I don't see a reason why you shouldn't do that for the other girls, too."

Gwen stood. She looked so much bigger when she was at full height. For a crazy second Robyn thought she might change into a wolf and pounce. Then Gwen calmed. The anger rolling off her simply disappeared. Her hands were still fists, and her face flushed. She cocked her head and said, "Has she told you to say that to me?"

"Who?"

"Some sick trick to get me to remember that night," Gwen said. "To feel guilty and come to your rescue?"

Robyn tried to grab onto something she could understand. "No one said anything like that to me. But that doesn't make what I've said less true. You could help. You just don't want to. Maybe it went wrong the first time, but the intention was good. You must have known that it was." She desperately tried to fight her corner. "Where were you that night anyway? No one mentioned seeing a white wolf."

Gwen's face was a mask of fury; all the color drained from her cheeks. But Robyn pushed further, and it suddenly hit her. "You weren't there that night! You left the Black Wolf alone to die, and now you feel guilty—"

The rest was lost as Gwen flew at her, catapulting both of them against the broken cabin door. They broke through it, a churning mass of limbs and hair, out over the porch to fall down the steps into the mud.

Grunting in pain, Robyn tried to stand up. A fist caught her cheek and floored her. She yelped and swung out blindly, but missed.

"Morganne! Her name was Morganne!" Gwen was yelling. Robyn ducked the next punch and kicked Gwen square in the belly. It barely slowed her down. Gwen was too fast, too coordinated. Robyn couldn't land a good punch. She kicked out wildly and caught Gwen on the side of her knee. Gwen lost balance, and Robyn quickly kicked at the knee again. Gwen toppled pulling Robyn down with her.

"Stop it!" Robyn cried. They lay panting in the mud. Robyn rubbed her bruised cheek, and Gwen rolled about, holding her knee and cursing loudly.

"Are you done?" she asked, turning her head to look at the big, strong woman lying next to her, chest heaving, yelling obscenities at the treetops.

"Are you?" Gwen snapped back, still nursing her knee. "You nearly broke my bloody leg."

"Aye. I did that, lass." She deliberately used Gwen's brogue.

Gwen chuckled. Then immediately grew serious. She looked up to the trees, to the little chink of blue sky beyond.

"Morganne found the girl. Greta, she was called," she said. Her voice dull and flat. "She found her one morning starved halfway to death. Morganne worked a little magic while I brought the wee lassie some food. We soon learned that there was a brother, out in the woods somewhere, to complete the pair. Morganne took pity on the girl. She taught her how to feed herself, and played with her in the woods. I think she loved the little rascal. One day Morganne asked me if she could bite Greta. I wasn't happy about it, but who was I to deny her, especially as there were not that many of us around here." Gwen fell silent for a moment; lost in memories. Then she shook herself and continued, "When it was done, the siblings went into your village and the years passed with Greta coming to visit us every so often. One day she came to ask for help. She couldn't bear the mindless passivity of the village girls, slaving away day and night, only useful for cleaning the house and opening their legs."

"Since Morganne had bitten Greta, I suppose she wanted to help the rest?"

Gwen wouldn't meet her eyes. Instead she reached out for Robyn's hand. "I was against it. I thought it was a reckless and stupid thing to try. But Greta lured her in, telling her that there was no reason not to help those girls when we had already helped her."

Robyn winced at the rawness in Gwen's voice. She couldn't disguise the pain this story and its memories brought her.

"Morganne was on fire for the idea. I tried so hard to put some sense into her head, but she wouldn't listen. I told her how dangerous it would be. I told her it wasn't any of our business. Why should she risk so much for strangers? But she said it was worth the risk, even if she only bit one single girl and brought her to her senses."

"Gwen, you tried, but you couldn't stop her. She wanted to do this."

"There was nothing I could do so I let her go."

"So, you never saw..."

"I saw all of it," Gwen whispered. "I was restless here alone. I couldn't settle. So I went to be at her side just in case anything went wrong. I was too late. He was cutting off her head with a triumphant roar." Her voice was indifferent, but her fingers shook in Robyn's grasp. "He wasn't even man enough to face her one on one. She had fallen into a pit. Her pelt was riddled with arrows. He must have stood and shot at her for some time. Then he hauled her out and beheaded her for his trophy."

Robyn felt sick. She remembered the matted head hanging above Hunter's chair at the inn. Knowing it was Morganne, her lover's lost mate made her stomach sour.

"I'm so sorry. I didn't know." She sat up slowly. "I would have never spoken to you like that, if...wait, did you say a pit?"

"Aye." Gwen nodded. "I heard the rest of the Riders approaching and had to go, or else I would have buried him in it. Much as I wanted to kill him, I didn't want to get myself killed while trying."

Robyn frowned. "He must have known. He must have heard them talk."

"What do you mean?"

"There aren't any pits magically appearing around here," she said, trying to remember back to the days of the Black Wolf. "Could he have followed Greta? At that time, we were all aware of his attraction to her. She was a new face, some fresh blood for the village breeding stock. A lot of the men were sniffing around her but she paid no attention, and that marked her out as odd. People assumed it was because she and Hans were not from the village though he fitted in as quickly as he could. Greta was always standoffish and strange. Maybe Hunter followed her to her meeting with Morganne?"

"You think he overheard their plan?" Gwen was skeptical. "Wouldn't that be a little too much luck?"

Robyn raised an eyebrow. "He is the Wolfmounter!" she said mockingly. "Yet he has never done anything other than lie, steal, and pretend. I think he has a bright, sparkling, lucky star shining above his handsome head."

Gwen's eyes glistened with unshed tears. "Let's say he already knew when Morganne would come." Her voice was thick with emotion. "Why not tell the Riders? Why dig a hole on his own?"

Robyn was restless with energy, so she stood up and started pacing back and forth. "The Black Wolf's death changed everything for Hunter," she said. "It made him the captain of the Red Riders. Killing a wolf made him the perfect man for the job. So he went out, dug a hole, and lured Morganne there. All these years he has pretended he had killed the wolf in a face to face fight in the woods."

Gwen took her time to digest this. Robyn wanted to take her in her arms, the hurt was so raw across her face, but she didn't dare go too close. Gwen needed space for the pain raging inside her.

"Hunter will eradicate everything and everyone in his way. He killed Morganne to become captain and rise up the social ladder. He tried to kill me for knowing—"

"Kill you?" Gwen stared at her.

"He was stupid enough to let me live, but he chased me away and told the village I was dead."

"Why didn't you say something earlier?"

She shook her head. "I told you I was banned. I didn't know Hunter had made up this story. And most importantly I didn't realize until recently that I hadn't done anything wrong. I thought I must have enraged him and that he was, in a twisted way of thinking, right to kill me for my misbehavior."

"Because that's the way you learn it from the cradle in your village."

Robyn nodded sadly. "It can't go on like this. We need to do something. It has to end either with or without you," she said. "If you choose to come with us, we go back into the village and continue where Morganne left off, by biting every single woman there. If you choose not to, then Rose and I will try and eliminate Hunter. In my heart I suspect we will only manage to help Rose escape. Anyway, I will be at the arranged meeting place two days from now."

"And get yourself killed like she did."

Robyn sighed. That hadn't sounded pitiful; Gwen had just stated a fact. She crouched before her. "I can't make her come back, but I can try to avenge her."

Gwen looked at her blankly. "Why?"

With a sad smile Robyn answered, "Because I love you, Gwen, even if you…" The rest trailed off because she wasn't sure if the ending should be, 'don't love me back' or, 'don't come with me'. When Gwen didn't reply, Robyn placed a kiss on Gwen's mud streaked hair. "Think about it," she murmured and turned away when icy fingers closed around her wrist. Gwen looked up at her.

"There's no need."

Chapter 11

Rose put her knife back in her boot, smoothed the dress down and pulled a cloth over her basket to make sure nobody could see the underskirt she was hiding there. She opened the heavy wooden door that led from her basement room up into the kitchen and was disappointed to see Hunter already at the table inspecting his bow and arrows. She went and waited dutifully before him until he acknowledged her. Another moment passed in silence before he finally greeted her good morning without looking up.

"I hope you'll have a pleasant day...brother." Rose had to fight not to choke on the word, so far she had managed to disguise her true feelings.

He nodded and waited for her to bring him breakfast. Good housekeeper that she was, everything was already prepared the evening before. All she had to do was throw some eggs in the pan. He cut his own bread, at least he could do that much for himself, and she thanked him politely when he cut another slice for her.

"My wife is still asleep, would you tell her I'll be late home tonight."

She wondered if he would ever be able to remember Whitney's name. "Of course. Shall I put some dinner by for you?"

"No, I'll have something to eat at Spindlefinger's." He lifted his plate for her to serve him eggs. "We're having a meeting about how to protect the village now that the trade routes are open again, and bandits are everywhere. Spring is a dangerous time. Spindlefinger should get his first delivery of wine at noon today if the vintner can make it past all the thieves on the road."

He praised her eggs. "You've come round faster than I thought." He gestured vaguely around the spotlessly clean room.

The fruit knife in her hand sliced sharply through the apple she was holding. "I have a good master to learn from."

Hunter leaned back in his chair and smiled smugly. His hands folded over his full belly. "Well, I always thought you needed more discipline to become a presentable woman. You were never as pliable as your sister, but—"

"The right man has finally called me to order," she finished his sentence with the brightest smile her churning stomach would allow. Her reward was a reassuring pat on her backside as she placed the neatly cut apple before Hunter. *I hope you choke to death on it, you pig.*

"Oh, since I won't be seeing you again today, is it all right to go to the edge of the forest for my herbs?" She tried to sound casual.

Hunter sighed. "Rose—"

"I know." She cut him short and placed her hand over his. "I promise to be careful, and I won't even go into the forest. The herbs I need are just past the North gate."

Hunter laid his other hand on top of hers pushing Rose's self-control to its limits, but she overcame the urge to sink the fruit knife in him. Instead, she gently rubbed her thumb over his knuckles. "I wanted to cook my potted rabbit for your dinner tomorrow."

His Adam's apple bobbed as he swallowed in anticipation. If she could do one thing, it was cook rabbit like a goddess. He always said it was the best he'd ever eaten, probably because Whitney couldn't cook to save her life.

"Your glistening rabbit?" he asked, almost drooling.

"Yes," she breathed. "And only the sage makes the skin nice and tasty the way you like it."

He gave in, she could see it in his eyes. "Fine, but watch your step."

"I will," Rose beamed and started to wipe down the kitchen counter with a slight sway of her hips like every perfect housewife should.

After Hunter was gone, and she had attended to Whitney's every need, Rose congratulated herself quietly for not setting the house on fire for yet another morning. Outside, the sun had risen high in the east, and she had to hurry to get her preparations ready for the plan to begin. Whitney was still upstairs resting her tired legs; this gave Rose peace to fold everything neatly into her basket before she left for Spindlefinger's.

Hunter and his men would be at the Rider headquarters to discuss routes and bandits, and other such men stuff, so she should have enough time for everything to run smoothly. Rose made her way through the streets, greeting the women at the market square who were busy opening their booths for the day. Casually she turned into the street behind the inn, casting a last glance over her shoulder before she slipped into the narrow alleyway where the deliveries to Spindlefinger's were made. As expected, the back door was locked, but the alley was empty of people.

Rose retrieved the picklock from the bottom of her basket. Hunter's basement was full of strange things he'd acquired in his line of duty, like picklocks, and daggers, and man traps. And since he never thought her worth the while he hadn't bothered putting them safely away before he'd dumped her down there to live. Instead, he had ordered her to clean it up and sort out everything. One task she had loved doing. The picklock had been her favorite find. She had used it to get in and out of the house many times in the beginning when she had first started searching for Robyn.

So her good brother had been useful for one thing at least. She carefully picked open the lock and slipped inside. It was dark in the stockroom, but her eyes adjusted rapidly.

The door to the main inn was ajar, and she approached carefully in case someone was working in the bar. Everything was quiet. No one was there. Perfect. The chairs were still on the tables, and the bar was wiped down with all the glasses neatly stacked on the shelves. She looked over to Hunter's special seat and took a deep breath. Rose had never known the woman who'd been the Black Wolf, even though she had bitten her and heightened Rose's senses to match that of her own. Now she stood looking into the hollowed-out eyes of the wolf's head hung over Hunter's chair as a trophy.

Greta had been Morganne's friend, and Rose could feel the rawness of her loss every time she was with the girl, almost as if it were her own. Perhaps the bite of the wolf did that, bound them all together, so they felt each other's grief and compassion?

Rose felt such anger at what Hunter had done. He had defiled a noble creature. She didn't know what had happened in the woods, but she refused to believe the legend of the fearless hunter, Wolfmounter. She refused to believe anything that came out of Hunter's mouth; he was a cheat and a liar, she knew this with all her heart.

Pushing up her sleeves, Rose got to work. She had to take down that head and hide it before Gwen saw it. When all women of the village were finally gathered in here, she could guarantee nobody would notice a missing trophy. Spindlefinger would be so busy counting his delivery of wine casks and trying to beat down the price, that he probably wouldn't notice the space above the fireplace either.

Someone knocked on the inn door. *Who on earth?* The knocking became louder.

"On my way," Spindlefinger yelled from above, and she heard his footsteps on the creaking stairs. Rose drew back into the shadows of the storeroom and waited.

"Ah, Captain, it's you. I've got them over here."

Rose whispered a curse as Spindlefinger ushered Hunter to the bar.

"Not that I'd question your loyalty to the Riders, but let me have a taste first." She heard Hunter say.

Spindlefinger sneered back at him, "Of course, you'll have a taste."

Curious at what they were talking about Rose crept closer to the open door to take a peek. Spindlefinger pulled a glass from the cupboard and poured Hunter a tiny splash of wine. She wasn't stupid, she knew that Hunter was bargaining on the sly with the food and wine sellers of the surrounding villages, how else could the Rider's headquarters be filled with the best produce. She settled in and waited, hoping the deal wouldn't take too long.

"It's a good vintage. I'll take two for my private use. My men will fetch the rest tomorrow." Of course, he would help himself. Rose curled her lip in disgust. "I assume it's at the usual discount." It wasn't a question.

"The usual." Spindlefinger ground his golden teeth together.

"Why so sour, my friend?" Hunter asked, a soft threat in his voice. "You should be proud to support the Riders."

The landlord wasn't going to be pushed around. "The taxes you spare me barely cover the free drinks I give you every night, Captain Wolfmounter."

"It costs us, one and all, to save the village from unruly beasts and vagabonds. Would you refuse my men a free drink after a hard nights work?"

"Unless I'm mistaken, there's still a beast to catch." Spindlefinger shot back at him. Rose could hear Hunter's snort of anger. Spindlefinger ignored him and carried on with the business at hand. "I'll have forty shillings for these, and the rest is for free, as always." There was a jingling as coins were handed over.

Rose sighed. *Now leave.*

"I wish you luck for the day, and hope to see you victorious and thirsty tonight." Spindlefinger started up the stairs. "You know the way out, Captain."

Rose tapped her foot; time was running. She couldn't wait much longer, but Hunter was in no hurry to leave. He leaned against the bar and stared over at his trophy.

"Damn beast," he muttered. "I'll catch that other monster and when I do, I'm going to burn it like I should have done you." He poured another cup of wine. Rose closed her eyes, praying he'd just drink and leave. Instead, he went over to his chair and sat down. Rose cursed under her breath. Then another knock came to the door.

Hans! It was Hans Sweets; she could smell him. Impatiently, she waited for Hunter to open the door.

"You're late." Hunter let him in.

"My sister detained me. We were baking pastries and—"

"You helped her *bake*?" Hunter asked incredulously.

Hans looked embarrassed. "I, well…I…We both have a liking for it and its fun."

Rose raised an eyebrow at these words, but Hunter didn't show any sympathy. "Don't let something like that keep you late for a meeting with me again, are we clear?"

"Yes, sir."

"Did you get the poison?"

Hans hesitated. He looked down at his feet.

"What is it?" Hunter asked tersely.

"I got it, sir," he said with a sigh. "The men are tipping their arrows right now."

"Perfect." Hunter's mood was lifting, Rose was unsure if it was because of Hans's news or the wine he was guzzling.

"Sir? Do you believe poisoned arrows are really necessary? I mean, don't you think our mere presence would be enough to chase off any thieves?"

Hunter was silent for a second and Rose wished she could see his face. "It's not a question of belief. I *know* how to protect my village, or do you doubt my judgment?"

The stairs creaked as Spindlefinger came back to his taproom cutting Hans's apology short. "Ah. Instead of bidding farewell to one Rider, I now say good morning to two red capes." He didn't sound happy. "I don't suppose you'd like to buy breakfast?"

Rose saw Hans dip into his pocket and throw a few shillings on the bar. Spindlefinger scooped them up and headed for the kitchen.

Rose's shoulders slumped. She would never get near the wolf head. She had run out of time. Maybe she'd get another chance before Gwen arrived. Disappointed her plan was already beginning to unravel Rose tiptoed out of the storeroom and back into the alley. She'd have to run all the way to the meeting place in the woods and pray that Robyn would be there waiting for her.

Rose kept on to the forest edge until she was out of sight of the village, then sneaked further into the trees. She made for the copse where she had met Robyn a few days ago and waited. First came the wind in the leaves, then the birdsong, and finally, from close by she heard a whisper.

Rose recognized Robyn's voice and nearly wept with relief when it suddenly occurred that Robyn wasn't talking to her? In an instant she was flat on her ass, her basket flung yards away from her, and fangs snapped inches from her face.

"Gwen!" Robyn hissed and placed her hand on the neck of the largest, whitest wolf Rose had ever seen. "That's Rose; she's on our side."

The wolf, called Gwen it seemed, stepped back reluctantly. Rose stumbled back onto her feet and dusted down her skirt with shaking hands. She looked them both over. Robyn in her trousers, her hair pulled back in a sensible ponytail, and Gwen, the white wolf she hoped would finally bring enlightenment to the village women.

"I'm so glad I'm on your side," Rose said. Her chest tightened. She had doubted there would be a side to be on.

Robyn smiled at her. "We all want Hunter to pay for his actions, and we want to make the girls see that there is another life waiting for them if they have the balls to grab it."

"And you'll make sure they'll get those balls, right?" Rose asked, looking at Gwen, who nodded grimly.

"So we're agreed. Everything can go as planned?" Rose asked. Both Robyn and Gwen nodded. Rose took that as her cue. "Okay, Robyn, if you would please strip."

Gwen growled at Rose when she came over to Robyn and removed the tie from her ponytail. She ruffled her long hair into a mess. "You've just escaped the claws of a great beast and have been roaming through the forest looking for help," Rose said, amused at Gwen's protective glare. "Your clothes are ripped to shreds, and your hair and face are covered in dirt."

"We know what we're doing," Robyn reassured her lover while Rose opened her basket and brought out the clothes she had stolen from home.

"Pull on this old underskirt. I'll hide your trousers in here," Rose said.

Gwen moved between the two women, blocking Rose's view of Robyn's partially naked body. Rose didn't quite know whether to laugh at Gwen's attempt to be a dressing room screen or be a little scared that she was big enough actually to manage it.

When Robyn was dressed she gave Gwen an expectant look. The wolf ripped at her with its claws, tattering the dress to ribbons. Rose looked her over with approval. "My, you do look as if you've had an adventure. Just one more thing." And she smeared Robyn's face and arms with dirt. "Shall we talk this over one more time?"

"I guess we all know what to do," Robyn said, looking at the wolf. Gwen nudged Robyn's hand, and she bent down to wrap her arms around her neck. She whispered something into a furry ear. Rose could have overheard the whisper if she chose to. She had perfect hearing since receiving her wolf bite, but she didn't want to intrude on Gwen's and Robyn's private moment.

"It will work," Rose said firmly. Her gut clenched. She knew what had happened the last time, but this was different. There were three of them, and Rose had thought of everything. With Robyn's help, the Riders could be lured out of the village, and nobody would come between the wolf and the village girls this time.

"All right, I'll go back to the path, and you will follow as soon as you hear the wagon," Rose instructed. "Ready, everybody?"

Gwen gave a last nod before she disappeared into the trees. Robyn messed her hair up one more time and squeezed Rose's hand. "It will work this time."

There was a slight anxiety in her voice that Rose would have liked to ignore, but she understood. She felt it herself.

"It will be fine. Now let's go."

Robyn took both their baskets and followed Gwen while Rose went back to the road and positioned herself. Hunter had said the wine delivery was due at midday. Rose hoped the vendor was a punctual man.

It wasn't long before she heard the clatter of a horse and cart on the cobblestones. She stooped and pretended to dig for some mint. Her bottom swayed in the air; she wiggled it a little more than necessary. Sure enough the vintner reined in his horse.

"Hey there, girl, what are you doing out here? Is there no work for you in the village?"

She turned around slowly, smiling brightly. "Good morning. I'm collecting herbs, my good sir."

He quirked an eyebrow. "Where's your basket, then?"

She looked around in dismay and gasped. Biting her lip, she eyed the vintner. "I must have left it in the forest."

He shook his head and looked her up and down. Inwardly Rose sighed as she fiddled indecisively with the strings of her bodice.

"I better go back and look for it." She inclined her head. "I thank you for calling my attention to it." She stroked her thumb over the swell of her breast to erase some invisible smudge while glancing nervously back into the forest.

"I'll help. A little thing like you shouldn't be running around the forest all by herself." He jumped from his wagon and gave her a toothless smile. His breath was stale from his wine.

"There is no need." And she so wished it was true. He was taller than her by half a head, so he wouldn't even reach Gwen's chin she noted with satisfaction.

"You're so good to help me," she said and pointed into the trees. "I gathered some buckrams from over there. I'm sure that's where I've left it."

"Lead the way, little lady." She could feel his eyes on her butt as she moved on ahead of him. "I'm sure we'll find your basket soon." His breath was too close to the back of her neck. "But you know, I'm my own master and nobody pays me for the hour I'll lose helping you."

Subtle, aren't we? She'd love to turn around and punch his smug face, but they needed him for their plan, so she curbed her temper and walked on silently leading him deeper and deeper into the woods.

When they were far enough away from the road, Rose stepped aside. A silhouette slid into view directly behind the vintner. She smiled innocently.

"I've just seen my basket. I think I can manage from here." She was surprised at how sweet-natured she sounded.

He clicked his tongue. "Do you need me to lend you a hand or not? I haven't time to waste."

"Oh, I've already got all the help I need, thank you." She was still smiling as Gwen grabbed him from behind and put her hand over his nose and mouth. He struggled, but Robyn and Rose closed in and held his arms. Gwen pressed harder, cutting off his breath. He gawped at them with fear filled eyes.

"Even though we didn't find my basket," Rose whispered, "I thank you for your help, nevertheless."

Gwen gave an exasperated snort and pulled the vintner's head back. He started to kick in his panic and clipped Gwen on the shin. She tightened her grasp until he slid to the ground unconscious. Robyn was already binding his hands and feet.

"Wait." Rose knelt and started unbuttoning his vest and shirt. "We'll need these."

"I've got my own clothes," Gwen grumbled. Rose looked up at her, raising an eyebrow at Gwen's leather trousers and leather vest.

"You hardly look like a vintner," she pointed out. "You look more like a hunter. You need to look the part."

Gwen tapped the man lightly with the toe of her boot and wrinkled her nose. "He stinks."

"Well, the least you can do is wear his hat."

Making a disgusted sound, Gwen looked at Robyn almost pleadingly. But Robyn shook her head. "You promised, Gwen."

"And you promised too, and you better keep it." They swapped hard glances before Gwen snatched the vintner's clothes from Rose and moved away. Rose wasn't sure what the standoff had been about, and there was no time to wonder. She and Robyn tied the unconscious man to a tree. His smelly old sock was stuck in his mouth to gag him.

Gwen reappeared as a vintner. The trousers were too short, and the woolen vest hung loosely around her flat belly while stretching too tight across her board shoulders. She looked disgusted.

"Here." Rose tossed her the misshapen, greasy hat. Gwen gave her a flat, humorless look before squishing it on her head.

"I want to get this over with. Come on," she snapped and led the way back to the horse and wagon.

Gwen sat on the wagon seat looking like a man, a grumpy, smelly man. Spreading her legs, she rested her arms on her thighs holding the reins loosely.

"Behave just like you do at home." Robyn tried to be helpful. Gwen raised a questioning eyebrow, and Robyn smiled back. "Speak as little as possible."

Gwen looked down from the wagon at her, and despite the grimace, her eyes were full of loving warmth. "If this doesn't work as planned, you run. Hear me, lass?"

"It will work." She sounded a lot more confident than she had an hour ago, and Rose hoped that this time Robyn believed in her words and that this wasn't a show for Gwen's sake.

"You *will* turn around and run, lass," Gwen ordered. "Did I make myself clear?"

"Yes." Robyn reached up and pressed a kiss on her lips. "Now deliver your wine, good sir, or Spindlefinger's inn will run dry. It is just a mile on down the village road."

Gwen sighed, and her eyes lingered on Robyn as she took up the reins. Her gaze dropped on at Rose. "Take care of her." It wasn't a request and Rose heard the undercurrent of menace.

Rose nodded. "We will play our part. You make sure that you're ready when we come running." *And please don't go into the taproom.*

Gwen snapped the reins, and the wagon rattled off toward the village.

"Ready to go?" Rose asked. Robyn nodded and gave a last look after Gwen.

"What did you promise her?" Rose asked, as Gwen rounded a bend and was out of sight.

Robyn didn't look at her. Her voice was quiet. "Hunter."

"Hans, you'll come with me on the north road," Hunter instructed, already in the saddle. They had to check the trade roads leading to and from the village for fallen trees, landslides, and other winter damage. A handful of his Riders had already headed south and east, and he would send Peter and the rest of the men west.

Just has he and Hans were leaving Spindlefinger's, the vintner had rattled up to the rear of the inn. That meant the northern route was clear, so Hunter decided he would take the easier route so he and Hans would be back within a few hours. That would give him enough time to sample Spindlefinger's new delivery before he had to go home. Who would have thought marriage would be so demanding? He had to take care of every little thing in the house. He had to ensure his wife knew her duties and kept away from him with that grotesque, big, fat belly. He wasn't sure how long pregnancy lasted, but he hoped she would get her beautiful figure back as soon as she had the child. He hated how bloated she looked, her belly, her breasts, even her arse was wider, for God's sake. He could hardly bring himself to touch her.

In fact, he was considering approaching Rose for a little fling. She had become such a sweetheart recently, thanks to his skillful handling of her. But he was too proud of his accomplishment to rut her. He wanted to show her off to a potential suitor as well-trained and chaste. He could get a small fortune for the captain's sister-in-law. It wouldn't do to pop the cherry on a deal like that.

Then again, and here his growing lust for the girl complimented his logic, he would need somebody to manage the household once his wife started popping brats every year. If she gave him sons, he would want her to concentrate on raising them, not wear herself out with cooking and cleaning. And Rose was free help. He didn't have to hire a maid with her tucked away in the basement. God, even his decision-making was hard. Keep Rose for himself, or sell her on? If his wife gave him sons he'd keep Rose, he decided. Too bad you couldn't know the gender beforehand. With a girl in her belly, there would be no need for his wife to take it easy, and Rose would be money in the bank.

"Captain," Hans pulled him out of his thoughts. He had a tight grip on Hunter's upper arm and pointed to the north wall. Rose came running up to them, behind her another girl in ragged clothes came staggering after her. Two of his Riders were already assisting her. One wrapped his red cape around the girl's shivering shoulders. Rose came directly to him.

"Oh, brother!" She was breathing rapidly from her run. "I'm so glad I found you. While I was collecting the herbs, I heard a cry for help." She pointed behind her to the girl she had found. Hunter followed her gaze and his heart nearly stopped beating.

"It's Robyn! I couldn't believe it, but she's alive!" Rose clung to his thigh. "Imagine! You do not need to grieve her loss any longer."

He slipped from his horse and went over to Robyn on unsteady legs. He had to see for himself. His hand searched for Rose's, who gladly took it and squeezed his in support. His life was over. All his threatening hadn't stopped the little bitch from coming back to blackmail him and ruin everything.

She stood before him supported by Peter. She was shaking uncontrollably, and her eyes were glazed and unfocused. With rising hope he realized there was a chance she had lost her wits? She was mad! Oh, Joy! Instead she reached for him with her filthy hands, clawing at his vest when he wasn't fast enough to step back.

"Hunter," she rasped through gnawed, bleeding lips. "I'm so glad! I didn't think I'd make it out alive, but the thought of you kept me going."

Was she feverish? What the hell was going on? He pushed back his panic. She crouched closer to him, and he had to stop himself from casting her off. "I know I have done a terrible wrong to you," she whispered for his ears only. He made an effort not to look alarmed. "And I've been punished," she continued. "Out there in the forest. By the beast. Please forgive my failure."

Madness. It had to be madness. He touched her sticky hair, making sure he looked emotionally overwhelmed, aware of the avid audience around them. Robyn pushed herself away and tried to stand on her own unaided. "I escaped the monster," she said loudly, so everyone could hear. "It held me captive, but I managed to escape. I know where it is!" she announced triumphantly.

Hunter froze.

"You do?" Rose pulled at his arm, clinging to him like a thoroughly frightened woman. "Oh, dear brother, save us all. Go and kill it!"

His mind raced, searching for possibilities to avert disaster. But he couldn't risk exposing himself in front of his comrades. *That was it!* He wouldn't be alone and unprepared in the forest, he had his Riders with him. They could do the work for him this time. Grabbing Robyn by the shoulders, he said, "Can you tell us the way?"

She looked uncertain. Tears glistened in her eyes. "I…I can try, I'm nearly sure I remember it," she cried.

"Poor thing." Rose wrapped her arms around Robyn. "Describe the way to the Captain, and then we'll go and clean you up."

He hadn't become the captain of the Red Riders because he was stupid. Rose was sweet and naive, and she wanted to help. But she was just a woman and couldn't see through the spiteful little bitch's plan. He nodded for his men to mount their horses, glad they were all gathered and ready. "Men, we are going on a hunt!"

Hans brought his horse, and he mounted. Robyn and Rose stood huddled together, with Robyn waiting to tell him the way to the quarry. He leaned over and grabbed her by the arms, swiftly hoisting her up in front of him. Robyn was so surprised she was speechless.

Rose looked on in shock. "But…but she's hurt. She's barely escaped alive from that monster, she—"

"Exactly." He cut her short. "And that's why the trail is still fresh." There was no way he would risk leaving her behind. She could corrupt Rose, or anyone who'd listen to her against him.

"Into the woods!" His order thundered, and his men wheeled their horses and galloped out from the village and along the road that led to the dark forest.

Hunter leaned into Robyn and whispered in her dirt smeared ear. "Lead me to the beast and maybe I'll spare your life. But you *will* leave this village. Do you hear me? You will leave and never flout my orders again." He hissed like a viper, even to his ears.

Gwen rolled another cask into the storage room and stretched her back. She stank. Usually, it didn't bother her, but this was the stink of an old, drunken bastard who had been lying around in God only knew what. She was glad she would change her skin soon. The hardest part of the plan for her was done. She was happily surprised when the golden toothed inn keeper waved her through without so much as a second glance. He'd shown her where he wanted his wine casks stacked and went off to check the paperwork she had handed him. It was lucky she had found it under the wagon seat.

As she trundled through the village gates, she had passed Hunter with Greta's brother. She had never seen the boy before, but his resemblance to his damned sister was so strong she knew she wasn't mistaken. And Hunter. Smelling him and not jumping for his throat required all her self-control. She wasn't good at self-control, but she told herself the plan was greater than her anger. Her thoughts were full of Robyn, and she managed to keep herself together. She would tell Robyn about it later. She would be proud of her.

"The papers are fine," Spindlefinger called through from the bar. "Do you want some lunch before you leave?"

She coughed. "As a thank you for rolling in your wine casks, or against the money you owe me?"

The little guy laughed "You're cleverer than your boss. Where is he, by the way?"

She hadn't said anything. "Sick. Winter brought the cold into master's house, and it hasn't left it, yet." The last cask lifted into place, she wiped her brow. The damned hat made her skull itch, but she daren't take it off.

"I'll have lunch." Gwen fully intended to take the money for the delivery, and while Spindlefinger cooked her food, she would check out the taproom. She needed to know the layout of the room, and see if there were any sneaky corners where someone could hide.

"I'll fix you some sausage," Spindlefinger said, and vanished into the kitchen. Gwen waited a second before she entered the taproom. Everything was prepared for opening time. The tables were clean, and the smell of cooking came from the kitchen. There were stairs to the next floor. That could become a problem later. Gwen did a slow sweep of the room and found herself facing the fireplace. Her blood froze. She stumbled backward and nearly toppled a chair.

Morganne!

Gwen closed her eyes and took a deep breath. Her mind had to be playing tricks on her. The Rose girl would have said something before letting her come here. She would have warned her. But Rose had said nothing. Gwen opened her eyes again. The wolf head of her beloved mate hung above the fireplace. She looked down on the room with empty eye sockets. Her beautiful amber eyes long gone.

Gwen felt sick, her whole body shook. The bastard, Wolfmounter, had killed Morganne in the most cowardly way, and all this time he had been exhibiting her head like a trophy. Gwen turned away and took a deep breath. Why had nobody told her? Not even Robyn had told her? She must have known. All of them must have known, and nobody thought it important enough to tell her? She rammed her fist into the chair, sending it skidding across the floor. She kicked it, then marched over to Morganne, intending to tear her beloved's head down.

"Are you all right, man?" Spindlefinger's words splintered the fog in her mind.

She stopped. Her body shook with the need to change and rip everything and everyone to pieces, starting by this filthy little imp who had allowed such casual cruelty.

"I...I..." She growled deep into her chest, feeling her teeth getting longer. Her muscles stretching.

Morganne was up there, watching her blindly. Gwen's heart threatened to burst inside her, but she was here now, and she had agreed to the plan so she could avenge her dead mate. She had agreed for Robyn's sake, also. If Gwen acted on her instincts now, she would not only get herself killed, she would place Robyn and Rose in danger. And she knew she couldn't lose Robyn. She couldn't bear such a loss again. She wouldn't let it happen this time.

"I tripped," she said quietly and felt her teeth retract. "Knocked the bleeding chair over."

Spindlefinger vanished back into the kitchen. Gwen righted the chair and sat on it. She still felt Morganne behind her, but it was Robyn she thought of now.

Rose stood rooted to the spot. How could she have been so stupid? The plan had been perfect! Robyn had been perfect! She had acted the weak little woman wonderfully. Everything should have gone as planned. Now here she was on her own while Robyn was in terrible danger when Hunter found out there was no beast hiding in the woods. Rose prayed Robyn would find a way to outwit the Riders. It wasn't as if she was a naive girl anymore, she had become strong and clever and could look after herself, as Hunter would soon find out. All Rose could do now was carry out the rest of the plan on her own.

She pulled up her skirts and ran to the market place. It was up to her now to gather the women together. She prayed that when the time came they would follow her directions without too many questions. Luckily, all the Riders had gone with Hunter, so she had only to distract the remaining menfolk who weren't already out in the fields or away at work. There wouldn't be much time, but she should be able to manage.

"Rose!" She turned to face Greta who was furious. "Rose, what have you done?"

She had to decide whether she could trust Greta or not. "Why are you here?" she asked.

"I heard the ruckus and ran over. Was that Robyn?"

"Yes, it was Robyn." No point in denying that. "She came back."

Greta gasped. "So you were right! She was alive all along. How did you find her?"

"At the spring feast. She sneaked back. I followed her into the forest, and we talked."

"About?" Greta asked hesitantly.

"About her winter with the huge white wolf," Rose said bluntly, hoping to shock Greta into action.

Greta was duly shocked but more than that she looked frightened. "She was with Gwen?"

Rose nodded. She took a deep breath and decided to tell her the truth. "We have a plan—"

"No."

"We are going to try again," Rose said. "This time it will be different. There are three of us and—"

"Gwen agreed? She's coming to the village?"

"Yes. This time she is willing to help. I don't know what Robyn said to convince her, but she agreed."

"It must be for revenge," Greta whispered. "The only question is on whom."

"Hunter." Rose hurried to explain. "Gwen only wants him."

Greta shook her head absently. "She won't spare the traitor."

There was fear in her voice, and Rose tried to soothe her: "I hadn't planned on pulling you into this. You shouldn't even be here."

"I'm not stupid," Greta snorted. "I saw you heading to the North gate this morning. I didn't think any good could come of it."

"You followed me?"

"Not really. I hung around waiting to see what happened," Greta said, looking grim. "And it didn't happen as you planned, am I right?"

Rose's shoulders slumped. "Hunter wasn't supposed to take Robyn with him."

"So in the end there's only two against the whole village." Greta shook her head, looking defeated. "This won't work, Rose. It didn't the first time and it won't now. I don't know how, but Hunter is always there to ruin it."

"He can't win every damn time!" Rose stomped her foot. "And you can't stand here and tell me it doesn't matter to you!"

Greta took a step toward her. "It does matter! It always did. I warned you to stop this before anyone got hurt, but you wouldn't listen. And what do we have now? A replay of seven years ago."

"Not if we do it right." Rose refused to replay that fateful night.

"How?"

"Gwen is ready, we just have to get the women into the inn," she explained. "The Riders are gone and—"

"Have taken Robyn," Greta finished. "She might die out there, Rose, don't you realize that?"

"Or she might survive," Rose insisted. "Meantime, Gwen must finish this."

"You could tell Gwen what happened. This time she can maybe save her mate."

"If Gwen went after Hunter in a mad fury the Riders would kill her easily. Robyn can handle herself. We need to keep going as planned."

Greta hissed. "We have to think this through now the damage has been done."

Rose put her hand on Greta's shoulder. "The damage is only beginning, and it will end today." She turned back to the market to salvage what she could of her plan.

Chapter 12

"Where to now?"

It was the third parting of the ways and Robyn opted for the right hand track again, leading them as far away from the cabin as possible. Hunter turned the mare to the right and came to a halt. "Hans, Peter, you'll follow me." He gave his orders. "The rest will go left. It can't be far now, and I won't take a chance and let it slip away in the other direction."

Robyn knew that wasn't the only reason. He wanted as few witnesses as possible. It had all gone horribly wrong. They had played right into his hands. Her only hope was that Rose and Gwen would carry on with the plan.

Though it was early midday, it was dark in the forest. The trees grew thick and closely together, their crowns shielding the light. The exposed roots and dense undergrowth forced the horses to a slower pace.

Hunter pressed his arm around her chest, pulling her tight against him. "I don't know what happened to you out here, but your not being dead is very inconvenient right now," he whispered against her cheek. "But fortunately, I can change that."

Robyn hadn't doubted for a second that he would let her leave these woods alive. She let him put his arms around her and pull her close. She let his mouth stray a little too close to her face. She ran her tongue across her teeth, marveling at how sharp they had become. Much sharper than those of other humans.

And she bit. She bit hard. As hard as she could, sinking her teeth deep into his bicep. Hunter squealed like a suckling pig pulled from the teat. He screamed so hard he startled the horses. In the momentary confusion, Robyn slipped from the saddle. The second her feet hit the ground she ran for her life.

Rose looked around one last time. It would have been wiser not to do this in daylight, but it was too late to change plans. It was now or never. She slipped into the stables. As expected there were only a handful of horses left. A lantern hung by the first stall, and she lit her candle from it, before opening all the stall doors and letting the remaining animals out. The stables were perfect. They were close enough to the East gate that people passed by frequently, but not too close to the houses and cottages. It was by far the safest place to start a fire.

One of the mares snickered at seeing the candle flame so close to her face, but Rose soothed her with gentle strokes. "Easy girl, you'll be out of here in no time." She brought all three horses to the door then took a last deep breath.

It just had to work.

She threw the lantern into the hay and waited to see the first lick of flames. The horses smelled the change in the air and started to get nervous. Rose waited for another second to be sure the fire had taken hold before she squeezed past the animals and opened the stable door wide. One horse jumped forward and fled. Rose slapped the second on the backside.

"Out! Out!" she yelled, and all three animals ran. Rose followed them to the market square.

The animals ran much faster than she did, but she knew a short cut to get her to the square first. The horses would arrive just as her panicked screams alerted the village.

"The wolf! The wolf has come!" She heard the cry before she rounded the last corner. Rose skidded to a stop. Greta stood on the wall of the well, head and shoulders above the villagers who gathered around her. Rose felt a lump in her throat. It hurt to see Greta betray her so openly. For a moment she saw only her lost friend, then her feelings turned to rage. Not only had Hunter almost brought her plan to naught, but her friend was sabotaging her last chance!

"We need to take shelter in Spindlefinger's." Greta's voice continued to ring out. Rose gasped, and Greta looked across the square to her.

"What are you talking about, girl?" Spindlefinger came running out of his inn. "I haven't heard a word about this. The Riders would be here if a wolf came through our walls."

Rose heard the horse hooves on the cobbled street behind her. They were moving slower now the danger of fire was behind them. She had to do this now. She had to act together with Greta and hope they were on the same page.

"I've seen it!" she screamed and ran among the throng of people waving her arms wildly.

Spindlefinger turned to her. "What have you seen, Rose Prospector?"

"The beastly wolf, sir," she said, wringing her hands, playing her part to the full.

"And why aren't the Riders guarding the gates?" he asked suspiciously.

"Captain Wolfmounter and the Riders have gone into the forest after the beast. He sent me to make sure you all hide."

"He didn't send a man?" Spindlefinger persisted.

"There was no time." Everyone knew Rose was a trusted member of Hunter's household. It was totally believable he'd send her in an emergency.

"Rose?" Whitney appeared at her side giving credence to her words. Now here was the Captain's wife to add even more weight to Rose's words. "Have you seen Hunter? Is he—" The horses burst into the square at that moment, and pandemonium followed. Women began to scream. Some men jumped to grab the horses while others cried out at the smoke slowly rising over the roofs of their houses.

"The wolf!" Rose yelled again.

"We need to hide!" Greta screamed, adding to the hysteria.

"The stables are on fire!" Rose cried out. "We need the men to protect us."

"My husband!" Whitney was loudest of all. "Why isn't Hunter coming back to save us!"

"They're all out in the forest looking for the beast," Rose yelled, happy as the voices around her got louder and louder.

"Could there be more than one wolf?" Greta added fuel to the fire.

It worked. Goldie put a hand on her husband's arm. "Please, Rump, you need to do something."

Spindlefinger leaped into panicked action. "Get the women to the inn. You men, grab buckets, jugs, anything you can find, and get over to the stables before the village burns down."

While Goldie herded up the women toward the inn, Spindlefinger left two young lads to protect them and took the rest of the men in the opposite direction.

Rose eyed the youths trying to order the women around. They were just as terrified as their charges. Those two wouldn't be a problem. Greta gave her a short, hard smile over the heads of the crowd.

"Oh, hold me, Rose, I'm so scared." Whitney was by her side, grabbing her arm painfully.

"Don't be frightened," she said and guided Whitney along with all the other women into the inn. "Spindlefinger's is the safest place."

"She can't be far," Hans said. He stood directly in front of the tree Robyn was hiding behind. She had to get away from here. Footsteps were approaching from all directions. She tried to weigh up her options. Staying here was impossible, but could she run? Did she have a choice? The three of them had bows, and she would be an easy target.

"You have my permission to shoot," Hunter said from nearby. "The beast has worked its magic on her and turned her against us. We can't risk that she finds her way back into the village." His voice was cold and ruthless. What a repellent bastard!

There was no other way. She closed her eyes and breathed in deep, holding the breath for a second before letting it out in an explosion. She pushed away from the tree and ran for her life.

"On the other side! Get her!"

She kept on running. An arrow hit the ground inches from her heel. She jumped towards a grassy hill, crawling up its steep face on hands and knees. She leaped a ditch. Only a few more yards and she'd be in the deepest part of the forest. *Run, run, run.*

Pain seared her side. So hot and hard that her sight darkened, and she staggered. The tearing of her skin burned through her entire body. Poison ran through her system, making her insides burn with heated oil. The stinking, foul fluid felt like it seeped through her pores, making her retch. Robyn fell to her knees, surprised at the wild yelp that came from her throat. She struggled to get up, but Hunter's heavy boot kicked her wounded side so hard the yelp turned into a scream. Robyn defiantly blinked her tears away and looked up into his sneering face.

"That shot didn't come from you, Wolfmounter." She spat on his boot. "Your hand would shake too much, you coward."

"No." He smiled. "That's what servants are for. Taking care of the vermin."

"So why has no one shot an arrow between your eyes?"

He crouched down and hooked a dirty finger to her open wound. "I wouldn't exhaust my good will, if I were you." He tugged at the gaping hole in her flesh.

Blinding pain swamped every sense in her body making her want to throw up. She convulsed in agony.

"Don't be so dramatic, my lovely. This is all your own fault," he spoke calmly. "I gave you a chance. I told you to run, and you didn't take it."

"Oh, I did a lot with your chance, you son of a bitch!"

He waved his finger, wet with her blood, in warning before her face, as if she were a naughty little girl. "Foul language is hardly an accomplishment." He tutted. "You shouldn't have gone behind my back. You should have stood by my side. *You* should have been my wife, not... not..." He frowned, struggling for the name.

"Whitney?" she offered, her voice dripping sarcasm. "I'd rather be dead than your anything."

"And you will, you will. Don't worry." Hunter drew his knife and stroked his thumb across the vicious blade. "You would have made a lovely wife. Pity. But maybe if I cut out your tongue you'll be a suitable housemaid. What do you think?"

Robyn hit him hard against his cheekbone with the heel of her palm. He lost his balance and fell backward on his ass.

"You little—" They scrabbled in the dirt. She tried vainly to be rid of the weight of him, but he pinned her down. She kicked his shins repeatedly, cursing that she couldn't quite reach his crotch. With her free hands she rained blow after blow about his eyes and ears, scratching and gouging until the cold steel of the knife against her jugular stilled her.

"You treacherous monster!" she snapped at him. "You've never been able to fight on your own. Not with the Black Wolf and not now, against a woman! Without your precious Riders you'd never have stopped me."

He had the nerve to laugh. Long and loud, and right into her face. "Idiot girl. You came to me, remember? Wanting to sneak your way back into the village and denounce me! But I won't give you the chance."

She tried to kick herself free, even though her side hurt like hell. Her wound was burning, and she could feel the wet of her blood soaking her torn clothes. She was damned if she died under him!

"Yes, struggle for me, my little kitty cat," he purred. His hand slid along her hip. "Maybe I'll take my time with you. My men have orders to wait until I call them. So we might as well enjoy these last moments together."

His knife drew a thin line of blood along her throat. She could smell the metallic scent. Fear was beginning to slow down her mind, blur her vision. She had to float above it and not give in. The wound pulsed disgustingly; she felt the throb of it throughout her whole body. She wanted to speak, but he pressed the knife hard against her skin.

"Shush, don't ruin our time together." His mouth was close to her lips. "I haven't decided, yet, if I want to get my trophy this way." He forced his leg between her thighs. "Or this way." The knife stung as it gently scored a new wound. "Maybe I'll cut your head off and hang it next to the first one? Then I'll go after the other beast and do the same. Then I'll have three." He giggled at his cleverness.

It wasn't fear for Gwen or even the finality in his voice that flipped the switch. Her body exploded in a ball of light and fire. The air around her whooshed into her lungs, and she rose as if she had wings out from under him to stand free and strong. The noise of the forest roared in her ears, along with Hunter's screams. But he wasn't screaming in pain. She hadn't hurt him...yet. He was screaming in fright. He was screaming because she stood above him on all four paws and growled in his face with huge bared fangs.

She opened her maw, intent on ripping his throat open with her new, sharp teeth when there came a terrible crash to her temple and then pain, awful pain. A heavy, bloody rock fell to the ground beside her, and she fell into darkness alongside it.

Chapter 13

A HEAVY CASK OF WINE blockaded Spindlefinger's front door, and outside the boys Spindlefinger left as guards barred the back door. The women huddled in the center of the room, comforting each other and their wailing children.

Rose eyed the door to the stockroom, hoping that Gwen was hiding in there and at least that part of the plan had gone as expected. She could feel the tension radiate from Greta's body where she sat next to her.

"At first I thought you were going to denounce us," Rose whispered, not making eye contact.

Greta didn't answer immediately. Instead, she sighed quietly. "I couldn't."

"I'm glad," Rose said and squeezed her hand as discreetly as possible.

"I'm not." Her hand was cold. "You know the story. You know who Gwen will kill first when she comes out."

"She won't kill anyone in here," Rose said soothingly. "You don't need to fear her." Even as she said it, she feared it was a lie. She had no control over what Gwen would do.

Greta was shaking slightly. "I can't change what's started. When will—" Greta stopped abruptly, her eyes huge. Rose sighed and followed her gaze. The Black wolf's head hung over Hunter's favored chair."You didn't take it down?" Greta hissed incredulously.

Rose bit her lip. Everything had happened so fast, and there was no time to remove it now. "I tried, but Hunter came in. As usual the luck was on his side again."

Greta wasn't listening to her explanation. "How long has Gwen been here?" Her voice was thin and quivering. Rose realized Greta was thinking the same thing as her, that any time alone in here with this grisly trophy would be too long. "Where is she?"

Rose looked around. The village women were becoming more nervous by the minute. Rose felt feverish. What had she done? Nothing had gone according to plan, but she was determined to make it work somehow. It was too late to do it any other way; she had to work with what was left. Spindlefinger was alive, despite having that horrible head hanging in his taproom, so Gwen had acted the part of a vintner, so far.

"She's in the stockroom." At least Rose hoped so. "Go stay by the door. Make sure nobody tries to hide in there after the wolf appears. I'll keep an eye on the stairs."

Greta looked at her as if she was mad. "You're letting Gwen come in here with that thing hanging there?"

"Is there any way we could stop her?" Rose asked harshly under her breath. "It's too late now."

"She will kill me," Greta stated flatly.

Rose shook her head. "She will help us, or else she would have raged like a tornado through this inn by now." Rose wanted to believe this, but she privately accepted there was no way of knowing what would happen once the door to the stockroom finally opened. “This is our only chance and we’ve got to take it.”

Greta narrowed her eyes and gave a terse nod of agreement. Hesitantly, she made her way through the crowd to the stockroom door and took up her place beside it. Their eyes met over the heads of the women and girls, and Rose knew they were thinking the same thing. Would Gwen still help them, or would she seek revenge on everyone in this inn? Especially without Robyn to rein her in?

‘Ready?’ Rose mouthed and Greta placed her hand on the stockroom door handle.

“Girls, please!” Rose drew attention to herself and away from the rear of the inn. “The men said we’d be safe in here. We must trust their decision.” She nodded at Greta. She managed to open the door barely a crack before it was flung back with a loud crash. With a hungry growl, a huge white wolf leaped through into the room. There was a split second of silence as the shock of seeing the beast sunk in. Then pandemonium brought loose!

The wolf turned her head and bared her fangs at Greta, who pressed up against the wall, fear written over her pale face. Everyone was screaming.

“It is here to kill us all!” Whitney shrieked. Gwen crouched to pounce though Rose wasn’t sure if it was at the women, or at Greta. The wolf’s whole body was tense and ready to fight. Rose could barely breathe.

It leaped, and the inn became a blur of limbs, and clothes, and sharp teeth. Screams and shrieks echoed throughout the room; women shoved each other out of the way, some tried to hide behind tables or crouch behind the bar, but Gwen found them all. She didn't hurt them. Rose could see she was careful with her fangs considering she was being kicked and torn left and right by 'helpless' women. Her tail was pulled, and her ears tugged mercilessly. She yelped a few times but was determined to finish what she'd started.

Rose saw the young guards peering fearfully through the window shutters. Ash screamed at them to help, but they were transfixed by the wolf racing around the room. A pitcher of beer crashing against the window pane snapped them out of their stupor long enough for them to race off in the direction of the stables. Rose looked after them, then back to Greta.

"There's not much time left," Greta said. She cradled Ebony on her lap. The girl had fallen and hit her head. The boys would call for Spindlefinger, and the rest of the men would hurry back to save their womenfolk. Rose supposed Gwen would be able to fight them off, as long as the Riders with their bows and arrows didn't show up. But it was too great a risk. Greta nodded at the door, and Rose understood at once.

Everything had gone so fast, and the women were too hysterical to think about rolling the cask away from the door and running outside. Rose and Greta pushed the way clear and opened the door wide to the afternoon sun.

"Out, out!" They yelled, hoping the women would run once they saw the path to freedom. Hopefully, the women would fall crying on their menfolk, slowing them down and allowing Rose and Greta time to escape. They had to be fast, and it looked like Gwen was almost through.

Rose helped a limping Goldie outside, feigning a limp herself, so everybody assumed she was a victim, as well.

"The beast will kill us all," another woman screamed, even though she was outside and already safe.

"It's gone crazy," Ash said. She was practically carrying Whitney, who clung to her for dear life. Looking at the chaos Rose suppressed a laugh. The women had fought back as best as they could. She hoped that indicated it wasn't a wasted effort and Gwen's bites would soon take effect.

Shouts were heard as the men came running from the burning stables, but they were still too far away for Rose to see them. She turned back to the inn to warn Gwen she had to go when the clatter of hoofs from the far end of the village made her blood freeze. Down a dark street, she saw the flash of a red cape. The Riders were returning!

Her fake limp forgotten she pushed aside the girls staggering from the inn and forced her way back inside. She stumbled into Greta, who was helping Ebony to her feet. Rose stopped a young girl and instructed her to take Ebony outside with her. She grabbed Greta's arm. "Did you hear them?"

Greta nodded and sniffed the air. "The Riders are coming back."

"You have to get her out of here. She still doesn't know about Robyn."

Greta stared at her. "And I should be the one to tell her?" she hissed.

"First we have to get her away," Rose whispered. "We don't know what happened to Robyn. Maybe she's all right."

"Or maybe she is dead!"

Rose couldn't play this game anymore. She grabbed Greta and shook her. "Gwen has to get out of here. Fast, and safely. You owe it to her!"

Greta ripped herself free. "I know what I owe, and to whom," she snapped.

Rose felt bad at re-opening an old wound and tried to mend it with reason. "I should stay and buy you time with Hunter. I might find out something that you can't."

Greta looked like she wanted to argue, but even she knew that Hunter trusted Rose more now than any other woman in the village. She wasn't happy, though. "Do you think Gwen will come with me willingly?" she asked.

The village men were almost on top of them, and the Riders were hot on their heels. Hopefully, the gates were still open. There was no time left. Gwen had to go.

"Tell her Robyn is waiting outside," Rose suggested. She couldn't think of any other possible reason. "We have to get her out."

Greta looked at her; fear and anger mixed in her dark eyes. "So first I'll be the decoy and then she'll rip me into pieces when she finds out I lied again." There was a dull acceptance in her voice.

"She doesn't want to kill you or she would have done so on first sight." It was a lame reassurance, but she couldn't offer anything other than her trust in Gwen. "You can explain everything when the two of you are safe."

"I doubt she'll let me get that far, but it doesn't matter. You're right, I owe it to her." Greta hurried over to where the wolf stood over the last few cowering women. She carefully placed a hand on Gwen's neck. The wolf whipped around so fast that Rose feared she'd bite Greta's hand off.

Greta pulled back instantly. She leaned down to Gwen's massive head and whispered in her ear. Immediately, the huge white wolf thundered towards the door. Rose barely managed to hold it open for them, as the wolf jumped out with Greta running behind, close to her tail.

Rose ran in the opposite direction to meet the Riders, squeezing out fake tears. They were headed to the market square. As she ran, she perfected her limp, for when she finally saw Hunter.

"Oh, Captain, the wolf—" Her words died in her throat as the Riders rode into the square. Two of them hoisted a heavy branch between them. On it, bound by its paws and with its muzzle tied shut by a leather strap, hung a big, red wolf. It lay limp and unconscious.

Rose's first instinct was worry that Gwen had seen this, but she kept her cool and played her part. Instead, she staggered with pretend exhaustion and fell into Hunter's arms as he dismounted from his horse.

"Don't fear, we've got it under control," he murmured.

"Captain, the beast it—" Spindlefinger came running up. He stopped, confused when he saw the huge wolf hanging from the branch. "You caught one, but the other one got away."

"Another wolf?" Hans asked before Hunter could open his mouth. He looked over at his captain, his face sweaty from the heavy burden he was carrying.

Rose shivered in Hunter's arms. He pushed her back and viewed her with eyes narrowed. Rose gulped, this time she didn't pretend. She had to make him believe her.

"It was a big white wolf trying to eat us all in the inn," she said, wide-eyed. "With paws as big as your head! I was so scared it would kill us all. I'm so glad you came back."

"How the hell did it get into the inn?" he asked Spindlefinger.

The man scratched his head. "I suppose the stupid vintner left the back door open when he ran in panic. His horse is gone though his wagon is still in the alley."

Hunter snapped, "Where is this wolf now?"

"It ran like a coward when it saw the red capes," Spindlefinger boasted. Rose did her best to not lash out at him. "But it took Greta with it."

"My sister?" Hans was panic-stricken. "It stole my sister?" His voice rose an octave.

"No," Spindlefinger shook his head and looked awkward. "She seemed to go willingly."

Rose didn't want everybody thinking Greta was a traitor. She had to be able to return home. "It must have put a spell on her. Don't these beasts do that?" Her eyes were as big as saucers as she looked up at Hunter.

He reached out and stroked her cheek. "Yes, I fear they can." He gave a grim look at the tethered wolf behind him. The regret in his voice almost sounded sincere.

"What are we going to do now?" Hans was shaken. Rose was surprised at the honest fear for his sister she could see on his face. Knowing Greta was alone in the woods must be horrible for him. Otherwise, he would have never asked such a blunt question of his captain. "I mean...um, what are your orders, sir?" he corrected himself quickly.

Hunter tensed. His dislike of the direct question was written all over this face. "Did it kill anybody?" he asked.

"No," Spindlefinger assured them. "The women are tending to the wounded, but so far there are only cuts and scratches. It hadn't the chance to do much damage. We kept it at bay until you came."

Rose snorted quietly. Not like there was much left for them to do after Gwen had taken off with Greta. Hunter believed him, though. "Put that…that animal, in a cage. And for God's sake throw a blanket over it, these women are hysterical enough," he ordered.

"Oh, brother, I need to go and look after Whitney."

He gave her a puzzled look.

"I haven't seen *your wife* in all this chaos," she said. "She must be with one of the other girls. I'll see her home."

From the glow on his face, she could tell he was embarrassed to not think to ask after his pregnant wife. "Yes, you do that and come tell me how she is." He let her arm go, and she ran as fast as she dared with a fake limp. She would circle the market and sneak away quietly into the forest. Behind her, she heard Hunter scream out another order, "Double guards on the gates tonight!"

Her heart sank. She would be locked in all night and unable to sneak off to the forest in broad daylight. She was trapped.

She was raging! Burning up on the inside!

Her eyes felt hot in her skull, a fine film blurred her vision. With the fire churning in her lungs, she should be able to blow that bloody gate apart. Again, and again she threw herself against it without success. It refused to be broken open. The way back into the village was barred.

As planned, she had fled, and the girl, Greta, had come with her. They were outside the gates, when, out of the corner of her eye she had seen Robyn dangling from a pole between two Riders, her red fur a mess of blood and arrows. Fur! She had changed, and without Gwen by her side.

Gwen howled and flung herself around determined to race back to the square, but Greta moved fast. She slammed the village gates shut behind them. The clever mechanisms slid the heavy bolts home. They were locked out. Not even a wolf of her size could break through them, no matter how hard she tried. And she tried and tried until her muscles bruised and ached at being thrown against the wood and iron.

"They're not following us!" the betraying little cur yelled at her. "We have to leave. Now, Gwen, now!" Greta was right, but she was asking the impossible, and Gwen hated her for saying it. For a second time, her mate was in danger, and this girl was in the thick of it. But this time Gwen would get even. They had run far enough in the woods so that no one would hear Greta's screams. With fangs bared, she leaped on the little figure pushing her onto the ground. Greta lay still as blood welled from the deep scratches on her shoulders. Her face distorted in pain, but to her credit she didn't cry out.

Slobber fell from her maw onto Greta's face. She pawed the wound she inflicted and this time Greta moaned in pain. It would be so easy to rip out her throat. Her teeth snapped inches from the exposed jugular. Greta froze below her, afraid to move, afraid to blink. She stared up at Gwen in pure terror. Gwen growled. She wanted to kill the girl, and Greta knew it, yet still she had helped her escape, and run with her into the woods. Greta lay still under her, accepting whatever Gwen would do without a murmur.

Gwen looked into her eyes, seeing the guilt and shame there, too. It oozed from her flesh, Gwen could smell the despair in Greta's skin. Despair for all the things she had done or had failed to do. Despair for that head hanging in the inn. The head of her friend. The woman who had saved her as a child. And now Greta was lying below her and prepared to die. Was this her way of making atonement for taking Morganne from her? Was that why she had accompanied Gwen out here?

Gwen's body tingled, and her blood frothed with the need to change. She pulled away from Greta. She needed to be able to speak. To scream in her human voice so this little bitch could finally understand the pain she had so thoughtlessly wrought.

"Gwen, I—"

With a scream, Gwen flew at the girl. Her midair leap beginning as a wolf, but when she landed on Greta's prone body, she was a naked woman. She didn't care; she swung her fist hard against Greta's face.

"Their blood is on your hands!" Her voice was still more the growl of the wolf than human.

"It was not my fault they got Robyn!" Greta cried. Blood ran freely from her split lip. "And I will not apologize for getting you out and leaving her behind."

Gwen stared down at her, but she was looking back seven years. "You have never apologized for anything. Instead, you choose to stay with those people when you could have come to me."

Confusion flickered across Greta's face. "You would have killed me."

"Aye, and it would have been the right thing!"

"It was Morganne's free will to help me."

"You lured her in with your naive words of freedom, knowing full well that she wanted a world like that." Gwen had still too much wolf in her system not to bare her teeth, even though they weren't terrifying anymore. "You could have tricked her. You could have dug that hole yourself, for all I know!"

To her surprise, Greta kicked her, pushing against her bare stomach, shoving at her shoulders until she forced Gwen backward and off her. Greta didn't try run, though. She scrambled to her knees but stayed where she was.

"I made a terrible mistake back then, and I am so sorry I didn't listen to you, but..." She took a deep breath and looked at Gwen straight in the eyes. "I didn't do it this time. I didn't bring Robyn here, and it wasn't me who wanted to repeat the chaos from that day. So stop confusing today with what happened seven years ago. It is done, and it was horrible, but we can't change it."

"There would be no need to change anything now if Morganne had just let you and your brother die," Gwen said flatly.

Greta looked stricken. "I know that if it wasn't for me, Morganne would still be alive," she said, slowly. Then went on with more determination. "But then, Rose would have never been bitten and made intelligent enough to send Robyn into the woods for you to find."

Gwen's breath came out in cold hiss. "My Robyn. My Morganne."

Greta hung her head. “Hunter has won again.”

“Get me back in there.” Gwen stood, willing herself to relax and not make the changing hurt more than it should. “Get them to open the gate, and I will forgive you.”

Greta looked up at her with huge eyes. Color rose in her cheeks, and a smile almost played across her bloodied lip. She shook her head sadly. “No.”

“No?” Gwen echoed in low, cold voice.

Greta straightened her shoulders and looked her square in the eye. “Every gate will be guarded by now. Evening is coming, and even at night they will see your white coat in the moonlight from a mile away and shoot you down.”

“Go back now and then open the gate later, and let me do the rest,” Gwen snapped.

Greta shook her head. “I will not risk losing you, too. Not if I can prevent it.”

“You will not prevent me from doing what I need to do when you’re dead,” she threatened.

“My guess is Hunter has already proclaimed me a traitor and your accomplice. The villagers will shoot me on sight. Maybe even before they kill you.”

The thought appealed to Gwen, but she didn’t believe her. “Your brother is close to Wolfmounter; I saw them together this morning. He wouldn’t let his right hand man’s sister be killed.”

“If he thought I had betrayed him?” Greta said dead certain. “In a heartbeat.” Greta looked away, her features betraying her hurt. “I don’t think Hans would put me above his captain. Not anymore.”

Gwen took a deep breath. Hans was a man after all, and his loyalty to other men was probably deeper than his brotherly bonds. "Then what next? Are you expecting me to turn my back on my mate?"

"Rose is still in there, and she has Hunter's ear. She might be able to do something."

Gwen shrugged. "Morganne bit her seven years ago. That should be enough time to 'do something'."

"Rose is clever. She not only survived Hunter, she also made him trust her. She will figure out a way to get us back in."

"Let's hope her cleverness is enough. We don't have another seven years to see if being bitten awakened those other girls from their slumber."

Chapter 14

In times like these it was essential to have a right hand man like Hans who thrived on blind belief, no matter what his eyes told him. Not that Hunter wouldn't throw him to the wolves without a second thought if necessary. Though it helped to know, the young man would sacrifice himself willingly.

Hunter stepped onto the makeshift podium his Riders had knocked together and positioned himself next to the huge covered cage. A crowd had already gathered. The village women were frightened and exhausted and looked to him for protection and reassurance. Their worn-out men stood behind them, looking up at him, Hunter Wolfmounter, with hope etched on their faces. His chest swelled with importance.

He coughed quietly, and suddenly everyone fell silent, focusing intently on him.

"Farmers, craftsmen, vendors," he began, "Riders of the Red Capes, my loyal friends, and their good women. I present to you, the beast!" He pulled the cover away. The wretched animal was almost too big for her cage, her bloodied, matted fur pushed out from between the bars.

There were gasps and astonished whispers, and a little bit of scuffling as the people nearest the front pushed back, away from the cage and its contents. Hunter hid his triumph behind a mask of concern for the well-being of his citizens.

"We, the Red Riders, have given our utmost in hunting down this monster. But meanwhile, unknown to any of us, there was another wolf among us. It crept in here this morning and caused panic. It even managed to corrupt the sister of our good brother, Hans Sweets. No doubt, it preyed on her weakness as a lonely young woman." A murmur ran through the crowd, and Hans looked very uneasy. He glanced up at Hunter, concern clouding his face. Clearly, this interpretation of events didn't sit well with him.

"But don't fear, good people. With the help of this ugly creature, we will lure the white wolf to us, and I will slay it like I did the Black Wolf before. I am the Wolfmounter, and I will protect you all once more." The reception to his speech wasn't quite as enthusiastic as he'd expected. The women were too shaken to cheer him, and the menfolk offered up little more than a collective rumble rather than the applause he'd hoped for. The mood of the people was dark. A wolf had entered the heart of their village and attacked the womenfolk. It was a wonder no one was killed! They understandably felt unsafe. He sought to reassure them.

"The gates will have double sentries," he said. "Riders will patrol the streets night and day. Now, let's attend to our injured and clean up the inn so we can celebrate." He pointed to the cage, "This is our first of many victories."

No one moved. The crowd stood watching him as if waiting for something else to press them into action. He frowned. He wasn't a magician with a rabbit up his sleeve! But he did have another creature to hand. He jerked at the bars to let them know he had it all under control, and that the monster within was no threat to any of them. The bitch was riddled with arrows; each dipped in the poison he liked to use on the winter vagabonds. It dispatched them nice and cleanly.

In the old days, when the bad harvests left scores of people starving, it was easier and cheaper to have beggars die in the forest where no one saw or cared. A death in or near the village meant a grave had to be provided and paid for. Hans hated the practice, but he'd had the arrows tipped as ordered. And a good thing, too. Hunter didn't think an ordinary weapon would fell a brute this size.

The wolf was so full of poison it surprised him it still breathed, but that was to his advantage, for as long as it lasted. He dearly wanted to put Robyn in a hole in the ground. But for the moment she served a purpose, and her time would come.

The crowd finally moved, and happy with his day's work, Hunter jumped from the podium, nearly straddling Hans on his way down. His second-in-command looked ruefully at the cage and shifted from foot to foot.

"What is it?" Hunter asked. He crossed his arms over his chest to add a little intimidation to his question. Hans was easily handled.

Hans straightened his shoulders. "I would never dare to question your orders, sir, but..." He looked down at his boots.

Hunter eyed him suspiciously. Never before had his right hand man said 'but' to anything he'd ordered. Of course, he could have just ignored it and walked away, but something in Hans' posture cautioned him to listen. If it was to do with his sister, then Hunter needed to hear him out. Any information could be useful.

"Well, speak up my friend." He tried to sound encouraging and not irritated. It took Hans a moment to formulate what he wanted to say.

"I wondered if it would be wiser to help her?" He nodded at the cage. "That poison is strong enough to fell a wolf."

Hunter eyed him. "And we felled a wolf."

There was more to it; Hunter could see it in the way Hans stepped from one foot to the other. "But if she changes back, won't she die? I mean, after all, isn't Robyn still one of us?"

"The wolf in that cage," Hunter said, in a hard voice. "It is no longer a girl from this village, and it doesn't need our sympathy."

"But what if she does change back? People will see. Will there not be questions?" Hans pressed his point. "I mean, she is obviously bewitched. Maybe Robyn really could tell us where the beast lives if she had a chance to recover?"

"How would she change again?" Hunter asked mockingly. "Her human side is gone. The other monster bewitched her and sent her back to lure the Riders into a trap. You have seen the women, seen what happened to this village the moment our backs were turned."

"Yes, but what if—"

"The transformation is over," Hunter interrupted. "That beast up there has nothing to do with the girl it once was. It wants to kill us; that is all. Therefore, it stays in the cage." He looked at Hans' mulish expression and tried another tactic. "Hans, do you think I would willingly hurt an innocent girl if there were any other way? Especially a girl I once held in my heart? "

Hans still didn't look convinced. "But what if there is a whole clan of them?" he continued as if Hunter hadn't spoken. "I mean, first the Black Wolf came. Then that mysterious white wolf, and now Robyn. There could be others. Lots of others. We can't dig holes for all of them to fall into."

Hunter flinched and narrowed his eyes. "What are you trying to say?" The slaying of the Black Wolf was dear to his heart. To his surprise, Hans didn't avert his gaze.

"I'm only saying that you were lucky to have the Black Wolf fall into an old bear trap," Hans said, "and were able to kill it on your own."

Hunter felt the blaze of anger race through him and struggled to damp it down. How *dare* this tubby little arse-licker question his skill as a wolf slayer!

"It took three of us to get that poisoned girl under control." Hans carried on, oblivious. "I'm only asking what will happen if there are more like her in our woods?"

"I am the Wolfmounter," Hunter said, aware his voice was rising. "I will take care of it when the time comes. Like I take care of everything else."

Hans blinked up at him, the doubt still in his eyes. Hunter made a snap decision. There was one way he knew would make Hans believe he was a good and decent man.

He looked away and schooled his expression into one of sorrow. When he looked back, his eyes held unshed tears.

"I lost my betrothed in those woods and nearly went mad with grief. And just when I rebuilt my life around my new wife, and we await the birth of our first son, my betrothed is given back to me. What do you think about that, Hans? Eh? And before I can thank the heavens that she is alive, she is taken from me again! It is black magic, I tell you!" He looked to the treetops visible over the village roofs. "I am the victim of something very evil in those woods. Something out there wants to destroy me."

Had he been too dramatic? For a moment he worried he had gone too far. This kind of spiel was okay for the women at Spindlefinger's who wrapped their arms around him when he told them about his first love. Of how he couldn't go home to his beautiful wife only to hurt her with the pain in his eyes. It seemed Hans wasn't that different from a bar girl. He reached out to Hunter and placed his hand on his shoulder, kneading it in manly empathy.

"I can't imagine how hard it must have been for you to shoot those arrows into Robyn. But my sister is still out there, and I fear for her."

His second-in-command was such a good boy. He would have to take his mind off his sister with some soothing words. "The girl will be fine. We are the Red Riders, trained to help those who are in need. We will save your sister and bring her back here." He placed his hand on top of Hans' where it lay on his shoulder and patted it gently.

Hans looked relieved. For the time being Hunter was safe, but he couldn't risk Hans questioning him in greater depth. "You know I consider you my brother, Hans. And maybe I made a mistake in choosing someone else to marry rather than your sister, but not all is lost."

"What do you mean?"

To bind Hans' loyalty to him completely would need more than just good looks and charisma. Hunter, regretfully, played his trump card. "We could still be brothers if you were to marry Rose."

"Rose?" Hans looked at him in surprise.

He gave the hand on his shoulder a firm squeeze, hoping he looked sincere. "I know you don't think yourself fit for such a great gift after questioning my motives, but let me tell you, I will forgive because I can't afford to lose my dearest brother."

"How noble of you, but are you sure Rose will agree?"

Now Hunter was surprised. Surprised that Hans assumed Rose's opinion even mattered? "Would that make a difference?"

"Well, I would like my partner to be willing to live by my side if it can't be for love."

"Love? What are you talking about, *by your side*?" Hunter felt the whole strange day slipping away from him with this conversation. Had everyone gone mad? "She will serve under you, that's what she is trained for. That is what *I* trained her for. I am making you a golden offer, and you question it?" His irritation was beginning to show, but he was too fatigued to care anymore. Hans was a buffoon.

"Of course not, my...captain. I will never question an order again." Hans sounded suitably cowed. "And you would make me a proud and happy man if I could consider you my brother."

"Very well, then let's get back to business." At last they were back on track. "What would you say to wolf on a skewer for your wedding dinner?"

The second night was almost over, and Rose still hadn't managed to get to Greta and Gwen. Riders guarded every gate and strode along the streets night and day. The whole village was waiting for the great wolf to finally come out of the shadows, drawn in by the smell of the wounded creature in the cage. Rose prayed that was never going to happen.

At night, the villagers cowered in their beds as Gwen howled and threatened, and chilled them down to the bone. To some extent it helped because the Riders didn't leave the village to go on the attack. Instead, Hunter wanted the beast to walk into his 'trap'. The more it roared and fretted, the more likely it was to succumb.

Rose hoped that Greta would know enough about Hunter's ways to stop any recklessness on Gwen's side. That's if Gwen hadn't killed her to avenge the Black Wolf. Had she been wise sending Greta with her? She had seen Gwen that day and known of her rage for revenge. She had failed to remove the Black Wolf's head and even let Greta run off with the wolf. Rose rubbed her face. She was exhausted. Greta was smart. She was alive and able to control Gwen, Rose decided. Or else the reckless wolf would have already stormed the gates by now, and died. Rose had to believe this if she was to have any faith in the future at all. Robyn was caged, Greta gone, and Gwen howling mad, and Rose felt she was not far behind her.

"You're up early," Hunter said, his voice raw from lack of sleep. He had been hurt in the fight with Robyn, even though he would never admit it. Rose knew because she had to make a poultice for his cuts and bruises. She also knew he was getting nervous because the beast hadn't shown itself. The whole village was anxious, and every hour that passed with no resolution looked bad on him. All the howling night and day was keeping everyone on edge. Rose hoped it pricked at Hunter's conscious, giving him sleepless nights and days of worry.

"Rough night, my brother?" she asked all innocence.

"Nothing you should concern yourself with," he said, brusquely. "Since you're awake already, make yourself useful and get me some coffee."

She felt his eyes boring into her back as she made his coffee. He hadn't done that in a long time, not since he tried to break her. She looked out of the window, at the lingering gray of the morning sky.

With the coffee ready, she turned around and placed it in front of him. Then she sat down opposite. Her fingers itched as if she'd touched poison ivy, but she knew she had to reach out to him, to reassure him.

"Rose!" The miserable howl from upstairs stopped her. She bit back a curse.

Hunter sipped his coffee, ignoring the plaintive cries. With a sigh she stood up, gathered a bowl and filled it with warm water and herbs.

"Do you need anything before I go?" she asked Hunter.

He shook his head. "Just make sure nothing's wrong with the boy in her belly."

"Will you be back for dinner tonight?" She fished for information. "Whitney is still afraid, and I don't think I feel safe either."

When his fist thumped the wooden table, Rose knew she had said it all wrong.

"Have I not done everything I possibly can to capture the beast? Have I not—" She put the bowl down and knelt next to him, stroking his thigh.

"Please forgive me, I didn't mean it like that," she tried to sooth him. "I only meant that we fear for you and that we feel safest when you're in the house with us."

He accepted her words and his knuckles grazed her cheek softly. "I know that only I can protect you, but I also have to be there for the whole village, too. So heed my order and take care of your sister, and I will be back before you know it." With a pat on her head, he let her go, and she went upstairs as she was told.

"What took you so long?" Whitney's whine greeted her when she opened her sister's bedroom door. Whitney was still in bed, her nightgown soaked in sweat. "The fever is rising, and I fear for my baby," she whispered brokenly. "Where is my husband? Was he watching over me as I slept?"

Rose tried not to tip her water bowl over Whitney's head. Instead, she opened the window shutters to the new morning. "You're not feverish. It's boiling and airless in here, and why you insisted on a fire, I do not know. You're asphyxiating yourself."

Despite Whitney's protests, she opened the windows wide and let the fresh air flood the room. "This will make you feel a lot better."

"Or it will kill me," Whitney argued. "And what will you tell Hunter when you have killed his wife and child?"

Saying nothing, Rose pulled back the bedclothes to examine the bite on her sister's calf. It was clean and nearly healed. Whitney wasn't ill, as she liked to think. None of the women were. Of course, the bites had hurt, but no one was infected or ill from them. Rose knew she and Greta had reacted the same way when they were bitten. Robyn had been different. She had pain and cramps, always worse at night, and in the end had been able to turn into the beast she'd harbored inside her.

"I'm feeling unwell." Whitney gave a feeble, fake cough.

"Dearest sister." Rose tried to stay calm. "I beg you. Get out of bed and wash yourself. You need to put on fresh clothes and go outside into the fresh air, like all the other women. You'll feel fine in no time."

Whitney groaned, and Rose sighed. She had made sure there was no fever or infection, and the child was all right. All Whitney wanted was attention. The attention Hunter never gave her.

After the attack, Rose had brought Whitney back to their house where she had insisted on waiting up for Hunter. She'd assumed he would come running home to check on his beloved wife and unborn son. Hunter had not come home until very late and Rose had had to deal with Whitney's fractious attitude. Unfortunately, Whitney showed no sign of change. She was still upset and determined to be a nuisance.

"Shall I send for Granny to have a second look at you?" Rose asked in exasperation.

Whitney's eyes lit up. "Yes! Yes. She will take good care of me." It was true. Granny would love to be of service to the wife of the Wolfmounter.

"All right, I will go and get her. Then I can get on with the housework while she tends to you."

With another heavy sigh, Whitney closed her eyes and suffered a little more to make sure she looked suitably ill for Granny.

Rose left the house and went straight to the market square, moving quietly through the empty streets. The village was still slowly waking up. When she reached the edge of the square, she took a quick look around. There was only one guard, Peter, standing by the cage. Robyn lay huddled in the corner, her eyes closed, her breathing labored. The arrows had been torn from her flanks, and her fur was dark and matted with dried blood. Even with the wolf's super-fast healing powers Rose knew the wounds wouldn't close quickly enough, there were just too many.

"Damn them all." She punched her fist against the market booth she was lurking behind.

"We aren't open, yet," came a muffled voice from inside. Rose jumped back, as the little side window snapped open. "Oh. It's you, Rose?"

"I'm sorry, Goldie," she whispered. "I didn't know you were in there."

"I couldn't sleep so decided to come down and get some chores done before Spindlefinger complains I'm too slow, again." She started, then looked at Rose as if she hadn't meant to speak out loud. "What are you doing here this early anyway?" she asked, trying to change the subject.

"I was on my way to see Granny," Rose said the first thing that came to mind.

"Well, you're going the wrong way, surely you know that?" Goldie's hand flew to her mouth. For the second time, she looked shocked to have spoken out.

"I needed some fresh air and decided to go the long way," she lied. Goldie was being very direct, which wasn't at all like her. She ducked back into the booth and came out through the side door to stand with Rose.

"You were looking at the wolf, don't deny it," she said. Rose smiled. This uncharacteristically brusque behavior was new for Goldie, and hope flared inside Rose. Could this be the beginning of Goldie's metamorphosis?

There was no time to dwell on Goldie's new attitude problem. Robyn wouldn't hold on to life for long judging by the state she was in. Rose had to act, and soon.

"I wanted to help," she confessed, crossing her fingers Goldie would understand.

Goldie raised an eyebrow. "It's forbidden." She lowered her voice to a whisper and drew Rose deeper into the shadows.

"But it's in pain."

"Captain Wolfmounter said it is dangerous, and it will kill us all," Goldie said.

"I know what he said, but what evil can this creature do? It can hardly keep its head up, let alone stand."

While Goldie considered this, she kept glancing back and forth between the cage and Rose. She looked uncertain and then surprised Rose with her next question. "How are the other women?"

"Sorry?"

"Has anybody died?" Goldie asked.

"No, they are all well. Why do you ask?" Her flutter of hope grew stronger.

"Because the beast is gone. It hasn't come back, and it hasn't killed anybody. And that poor creature over there," she pointed toward the cage, "had nothing to do with any of it. It is up there as a lure for the other one," Goldie said.

"Have you ever thought why the white wolf would come back after the caged one?"

Goldie gave her a puzzled look.

"Do you think it feels the pain of this one?" Rose asked. She wanted Goldie to think about it.

"You mean they are connected?"

"Why else should the beast come back here if not to save its mate?"

"You think they are mates? And the Captain knows?" Goldie was appalled.

"Why else put it on display? And at this side of the market square where the wind will carry the scent far into the woods?"

Goldie thought about it, really thought for herself, and Rose bit her tongue not to cheer out loud.

"So if we help this one, maybe the beast outside would know we are taking care of its mate and will stop howling for it?"

Well, that wasn't quite the outcome she had hoped for, but Rose would take anything she could get to save Robyn from dying in that cage. "I think so, yes."

"Fine, how can I help?" Goldie was so matter-of-fact that Rose blinked, not entirely sure she'd heard her right. Goldie stood before her, hands on hips, ready for action.

"I have to get to it and clean its wounds at the very least," Rose said. "It also needs water and something to eat. And, well, it would be good if Peter didn't notice us."

"You don't think we could smuggle it out?"

Rose's mouth hung open. This new, spirited Goldie was taking her breath away. "That would be too risky," Rose said with regret. "The gates are guarded and the wolf can't run in the state it's in."

"You're right," Goldie agreed. "Let's do what we can. I'll get some food from the inn, and you take care of Peter. Maybe you have some herbs that will put him to sleep?" Goldie didn't wait for an answer, she turned and headed back to the inn leaving Rose staring after her wide-eyed. Gwen's bite had worked! She could hardly believe it.

There was little time left before the first of the traders started opening up their market stalls; she had to hurry. With her basket held tightly before her, she headed toward Peter. "Good morning, Peter."

The boy looked down from the stage. He looked tired and started at her approach as if he hadn't noticed her at all. "Oh, Rose," he said, "you're up early."

"I'm on my way to Granny's house. Have you been up there for long?"

He shrugged. "I'm on the night watch."

"I've cut up some apples for Granny. Do you want one to start the day?"

He eyed her suspiciously, but she was the captain's sister-in-law and hadn't been a troublemaker for some time now, so he probably saw her as a respectable village woman.

"I'm not off duty for a few minutes, but ..." he hesitated and glanced at the wolf.

"Shouldn't the beast stay alive to lure the other one in?" She took the opportunity to ask. Then worried she'd been too forward when Peter gave her a curious look. "I mean, I'm probably naive but I just—"

"No." He cut her short. "The Captain probably doesn't care if she dies—"

"She?" Rose could have kicked herself for asking that out loud. Peter took a step back from the cage and shook his head. He seemed annoyed with himself.

"If you have something to feed it, go ahead." He spoke brusquely.

As if on cue Goldie came around the corner with a small piece of meat and a bowl of water in her hands. Peter looked from her back to Rose and raised an eyebrow.

"Thank you, Peter. Just a tiny bit, so she survives," Rose said.

"I'll go over here and keep an eye out for my relief. With my back to the cage," he added pointedly.

Goldie handed her the food. "What is that all about?" She watched Peter stalk away.

"I don't know," she whispered back. The hair on her neck stood on end, she almost expected Hunter to appear behind her and grab her by the throat. But nothing happened. The square was still deserted; no one else was around. Rose crouched close to the cage; Goldie hunkered down next to her. Robyn's eyes were closed, her breathing shallow. She was shivering, but at least she had stopped bleeding; there was no fresh blood pooling beneath her.

Rose pushed the scraps of meat through the bars, but the bowl was too big to fit.

"I'm sorry," Goldie whispered more to the wolf than to Rose. "I couldn't find anything smaller."

"You have to eat, darling," Rose said in a low voice so Peter wouldn't hear. The wolf opened her eyes at the sound of Rose's voice but didn't move. "No dying on me, okay?" Rose whispered with a sad smile. "I'm so sorry."

"You need to drink." Goldie poured water into her cupped hand and reached inside the cage. The wolf eyed Rose, who didn't know what other to do than nod encouragement. Slowly, the shaggy mouth opened, and a huge pink tongue lolled out to lap some water from Goldie's hand.

"You should go." Peter's hiss came from the other side of the stage.

Rose and Goldie looked at each other; the meat was still uneaten, and the wounds hadn't been tended to. The wolf lapped more water from Goldie's hands and with her claws slid the meat in under her belly to hide it. There was no time for her to eat it now, but this was better than nothing. Rose and Goldie had to go.

"We'll be back soon to help you." And it wasn't Rose who'd said it.

Chapter 15

It hurt.

Breathing hurt. Swallowing hurt. Even the sun warming her fur hurt. There were voices around her, but she couldn't make one out from the other. They all merged into a blur of mumbles and whispers, and sometimes a snarl. Her insides rumbled and she felt wretched to the bone. The hunger pangs passed, but her mouth was dry, and she couldn't gather any saliva. With shaking limbs, she tried to turn onto her other side. It didn't work. Her body convulsed so hard she thought she would shatter. Pain burned behind her eyes. Her chest blazed with each breath as the poison crept out of her. Agonizingly slowly, it burned its way through her skin. Her infected blood boiled in her veins, making her whole body shake with pain.

It hurt.

She tried to scream, but her mouth was not her mouth. Instead, it was a wolf's muzzle, and wolves didn't scream. And then, suddenly she could. Her scream rang hard in her ears. Her hands tingled, her legs cramped until she thought the bones would break. She imagined a knife flaying her open, and as she arched in agony, her body reared up and absorbed the wolf's fur down through her pores and home again, under her skin.

Her naked body slumped to the ground. Her torn flesh shivered against the cold metal of the cage bars. She was a human girl again, and it felt far, far worse than the time she had spent in her wolven body because now there was nothing, not even fur, to protect her anymore.

Three days had passed, and Hunter couldn't believe the white wolf hadn't attacked yet. The nerve-racking howling outside continued night and day until the villagers were half mad with the sound. Robyn was getting weaker by the hour, and if she died it would be okay with him, but then he would have to go out into the woods and hunt the beast in its own territory. His plan was brilliant, why couldn't the creature do what it was supposed to, and break through the damn walls so his Riders could shoot it down? To hell with it! To hell with them all!

Granny had been around all evening, taking care of his wife, while Rose had been busy with her domestic duties. Not even Hans had wanted to drink with him; he was so worried about his stupid sister. Secretly, he was glad he had not married Greta, and a little sad that he had promised Rose to Hans. He would miss her little round butt dancing about in front of him when she cooked.

Taking off his red cape, Hunter entered his headquarters with a sigh. His men were tired of waiting, and sooner or later he would have to present another plan for ridding the forest of the beast. When Robyn died he'd need another plan, and quick.

No sooner had he sat down when the door burst open. Peter pushed through the men crowded around the hall and came to a halt before him.

"It's happened," he said breathlessly.

"What has happened?" The boy needed a lesson in respect, especially toward his captain.

"Robyn," he whispered. "She's changed back." Hunter was on his feet and through the open door before Peter had finished talking.

People were already gathering around the stage in the market square. Most of them were women, and a few Riders had already formed a line between them and the cage. Hunter climbed up and took a look for himself. She lay naked, her long hair matted with dried blood, her eyes encrusted and closed, and she was shivering violently.

"Why, it's Robyn," a woman's voice came from the crowd. She sounded startled at the discovery.

"Robyn? Our Robyn? You mean she's not dead?" another woman asked. An unhappy murmur ran through the crowd, and Hunter began to worry.

"Did he know?" He heard another question asked, this time it held an edge of anger. His guts began to squirm. This was the last thing he needed.

"Good people, I pray you, be silent," he said and raised his arms. "That girl in there, she isn't the Robyn you know anymore."

"But she's hurt!" Someone dared interrupt him.

"She needs help," another village woman called out. He had told them to be silent, why wouldn't these stupid bitches do as he said?

"Let me tell you, it may look like her, but this isn't my beautiful betrothed anymore! The beast has magically brainwashed her. It has turned her into one of its own." The people fell silent, seeming to think about his words, so he pushed his advantage. "She would kill every single one of you if we let her out. Don't you see? It's a trick!"

A ripple of fear ran through the crowd.

"Did you know it was Robyn, all along?" called a voice that sounded vaguely familiar, but he couldn't place it.

"She will be kept in this cage as long as I see fit. And we will get that beast out there, too!" He ignored the question. Now he had the villagers' attention it was time to take control. "Riders, guard her!" He strode imperiously from the stage.

The crowd surged forward to take a closer look at the caged bird, but the Riders stood their ground and held them back.

"This is not going well, Captain." Hans stood before him.

"Why not?" he tried to sound calm. "Get up there and guard the beast. Everything will be fine."

"There is no beast, sir. Only Robyn. You can't let her die in that cage."

Talking back? His Hans? Hunter subdued the urge to slap his face. "If she dies, then we will find other ways to kill the animal outside our gates," he said instead.

"And how do you explain that to the villagers?" Hans was not going to go away.

Hunter dismissed that with the wave of his hand. "What's there to explain? She is the enemy; she has to die one way or another."

Hans took a step back. "You said she wouldn't change back and that she isn't one of us anymore. But now she has. You can't let her die up there like an animal!"

Hunter blinked. Had Hans just got louder? "I can and I will!" he said. "I am your captain and I know what's best for this village. I do my best to protect it."

"And what about my sister?" Hans asked with his arms crossed. "She is still out there. What are you doing to protect her?"

"If she turns out to be anything like Robyn, we will have to kill her, too," he said, bluntly.

Hans looked at him, for once his eyes weren't full of wonder and praise, but with trouble and uncertainty. "You wouldn't kill my sister."

Hunter hadn't time to nurse this bruised puppy. "Your sister hasn't come back yet. The beast has either killed or bewitched her by now. That's if it hadn't done so already? Why else do you think Greta disappeared with it?"

Hans looked aghast. "Robyn is badly wounded and I did that to save you. As our captain, you promised always to protect the people. But that," he said, pointing at the cage, "is not protection. And now you say my sister is conspiring with this evil in the woods?"

"Why," Hunter said, a plan beginning to form in his mind, "maybe it was Greta all along. She was always going to the woods. Who knows who or what she met there. I blame myself. I should have chastised her and made her stop, but she was your sister." He was enjoying this game. Hans was annoying him an incredible amount, let him squirm. Hans eyed him warily. Hunter wasn't used to getting looks like that from his subordinates. Hans needed to remember his place.

"Hunter, my sister is a good girl! We can't leave her out there to die." Hans had never uttered his first name so harshly.

"Don't take that tone with me," Hunter snarled. "Your sister's already dead, or as good as." He turned to go. He would deal with Hans' impropriety later.

Rose had never been more thankful for her enhanced hearing since she'd been bitten. She had seen Robyn change back and together with Goldie had gathered as many women as possible to see the wonder. She had tried to look as shocked as all the other women. Heaven forbid she should have known anything about it beforehand! But asking Hunter if he had known who was behind the furry mask of anonymity had made the crowd run wild. The women were arguing, really arguing, with the Riders who tried to keep them from the cage.

"She needs help!" Some women tried to squeeze past the Riders who firmly held their ground. "You're heartless monsters, let us pass." The shouts were becoming louder and the guards more and more uncomfortable. "As far as you're concerned, we could all be locked away up there."

Rose waited for the first opportunity to slip up to the cage and open the door, but the dispute between Hans and Hunter had distracted her.

Hunter strode off, leaving Hans to look at her in shame. It must hurt him deeply for his lover's quarrel with his darling captain to be overheard by her, of all people. Rose suppressed a smile and sidled up to him.

"You shouldn't be here, Rose," he said, reluctantly.

She didn't think there would be another chance to try and get him on her side. She plunged in feet first. "You knew that it was Robyn up there all along, didn't you?" she asked.

He flinched and nodded sadly. "She was under the beast's spell and tried to flee and then—"

"She changed, and like the good dogs you are, you shot her to bits to save your precious captain's ass." Rose was disgusted.

Hans looked contrite, and Rose realized it mattered to him what she thought of him.

"We wanted to present a beast so the villagers could feel safe," he said. "Captain Wolfmounter promised to kill her humanely afterward. But when we came back to the village he heard of the attack, and suddenly there was another beast out there."

"And you think Hunter would show her mercy? Like he did with the Black Wolf?" Rose kept pressing him with hard questions.

He tried to argue. "The Black Wolf has killed—"

"Nobody, Hans, it killed nobody. It caused the village no harm whatsoever."

"But it wanted to." He grew stubborn.

"Like the white wolf? Like Robyn? Did they kill anyone?"

"No, but they would have if it weren't for the Captain."

"The same captain who would never stand by and let a villager die, eh?" She looked pointedly at the cage.

Hans' mouth opened and closed. He couldn't seem to find any words. Rose took a chance while his defenses for his precious captain were down. "Greta is your sister. She has done everything for you, and now you put his life over hers?"

He was torn, she could see it in his eyes. She pushed home her point. "We have to help Robyn if we are to save Greta."

"*I* will help." The shout came from behind. She turned to find Peter. "The captain has lied to us, Hans. He told us it was for the best to take her back to the village, and look what happened. He doesn't care whether she lives or dies. Or even if your sister lives or dies, too. He only wants to get the beast and anybody in his way will suffer."

Rose wanted to kiss him; it was the first time in her life she felt gratitude toward the male sex. Peter understood what was going on, and was prepared to go against orders for the sake of a woman he barely knew. She had never seen such a thing.

"You're right, Peter, it is time to end this," Hans said.

Peter went first, helping Rose up onto the stage. Hans followed and retrieved the key from a pocket in his red cape.

"How dare you disobey my orders!" Hunter appeared from nowhere. His bow and arrow were leveled at Robyn, who lay drifting in and out of conscience. "That thing has to die; it is not human. It needs to be killed along with the animal it brought down on us!"

Hans and Peter stood immobile before the cage, protecting Robyn with their bodies. Rose stood to the side, unable to move, certain if she did she'd be shot. She had no doubt Hunter was so wound up he'd shoot at anything that so much as twitched. His eyes were wide and feverish. He did not look like a man in control.

"Nothing was brought down on us!" a woman's voice screamed. A stone flew from out of the crowd and hit Hunter on the hand. He yelped and dropped his bow. Goldie pushed past the line of Riders and started yelling, "The beast out there doesn't want to kill us, it's calling for its mate!"

"It tried to eat you alive in my inn, woman," Spindlefinger shouted. "Now shut up!"

Goldie didn't shrink as her husband tried to grab her. "This is Wolfmounter's doing!" she called out again, in a loud, clear voice. "He wants us to think the beast is dangerous, but it's never killed anyone! It could have easily ripped us to shreds in the inn, but it didn't. It had lost its mate and went looking for her. It is probably mad with grief."

Rose listened in disbelief. All right, the last part was a little hammed up, but it worked according to the uproar around her. Everyone seemed to be yelling now.

"Yes. It didn't kill anyone seven years ago, and it hasn't now! It only wanted to help its mate!" Someone else took up the call.

"Silence her!" Hunter shouted. Two of the Riders grabbed for Goldie. The other Riders burst through the crowd of angry women who screamed and yelled and slapped their hands away. Stones began to fly. Rose ran over to Hans and Peter, who both looked uncertain as to whether to follow Hunter's orders. More stones flew onto the stage.

She grabbed Hans by the arm: "Do you trust me to end this?"

He couldn't look her in the eyes, but Peter nodded. "Yes!" he said.

Rose fixed on Hans. "Please agree, if only for your sister's sake," she said. "You must go to the North gate, tell them the captain ordered it to be opened."

He gawped at her. "Then the wolf will—"

"No." She shook her head. "It only wants its mate back, just like Goldie said."

He looked her square in the eye. "Are you sure of that?" Rose took a deep breath. She would have never expected Hans Sweets would ask for her opinion ever, never mind listen to her advice.

"Yes, I swear no innocent will be hurt."

He pressed his hand to hers then sprang from the stage in a running leap. Rose turned to Peter. In her hand, she held the key to Robyn's cage.

Chapter 16

Rose's hands shook as she opened the cage. She reached for Robyn. "Stand up, Robyn, darling, we must hurry."

Peter handed her his red cape to cover Robyn's nudity. "Quickly." His voice was urgent. "There's not much—"

"Get away from her!" Hunter's yell was close to Rose's ear. She managed to duck as Peter flew over her head to land on the cobblestones below. He lay motionless, blood spilling from his face.

"Peter!" Rose screamed. The boy groaned and crawled up on his hands and knees. Rose had barely time to register he was okay before Hunter set upon her. She screamed, but there was no one to help. The market square below was a chaos of screaming, grappling women. They clawed at the faces of the Riders, dragged at their cloaks, and some even threw stones at them. When their husbands and fathers tried to intervene they soon hobbled away with kicked shins, and worse! It was as if a madness had possessed the village and its women in particular.

The guards from the gates came running on Hans orders, to support their brothers, but the women were like wild animals, clawing and biting anyone who so much as touched them.

Hunter grabbed at her and pulled her away from the cage. “You witch!” He howled into her face. “I trusted you! I made you my sister. I made you a decent, man-fearing woman! And this is how you thank me?” He gestured at the hell broken loose around them.

Rose smiled, despite her fear. “Why, brother, aren’t you happy with my present? Maybe I could give you another one?” Her knee hit home. He roared like a wounded bull and let go of her to cradle his groin. Rose ran over to Robyn, who had managed to crawl most of the way out of the cage.

“You’ll be all right,” Rose whispered,”I promise.” She was worried. She had to navigate a way out for them through this battlefield.

“Rose,” Robyn whispered, her voice dry and weak. She pointed, her face a mask of dismay at something behind Rose. Rose turned, but it was too late.

“I said get away from the cage!” Hunter grabbed Rose by the throat. With his other hand, he yanked Robyn out by her hair. “If you don’t want to listen, then find out the hard way.” His growl was wet against Rose’s ear, before he tossed her head first, into the cage.

Something wasn’t right.

Gwen paced up and down, not caring how much noise she made. Three days had passed, and still nothing. Greta had promised, and her promises had failed Gwen, yet again. Even though she knew Greta was right, and that charging blindly at the gate would get them both killed, the uncertainty was destroying her just as much as a hail of arrows would. She couldn't even voice her anger because changing back into a human would cost her too much energy, and she'd need every ounce as soon as she got back into the village.

"Rose will have done something by now," Greta assured her. Though she was careful to keep her distance. The girl wasn't stupid, she knew Gwen was seething.

Gwen growled low in her throat. There was turmoil in the village, she could hear it growing, getting louder. Greta stood up and closed her eyes, listening to the wind. Gwen's super-keen hearing heard metal grinding against wood. The gates were opening! Where the Riders finally coming to hunt them down? Perhaps Wolfmounter had tired of waiting for the wolf that would never come? They listened carefully, human and wolf ears straining in the wind, eliminating all other forest sounds, but the men approaching. Something was wrong. There were not enough horses.

"I only hear one horseman," Greta said, confirming Gwen's thoughts. What was a single Rider doing out here? Was it a trap?

Greta shimmied up a tree to check along the deserted road to the village. "The gate is open," she confirmed incredulously.

A trap. It had to be a trap. Gwen was certain of it, except the wind was charitable, and she couldn't smell another human anywhere near. Only this one rider.

"It's Hans," Greta said and clambered down from the tree.

Greta's brother? Gwen growled. Hans Sweets was Wolfmounter's second-in-command and his closest friend. So, it was a trap after all.

"I don't know about that," Greta said as if Gwen had spoken out loud.

With his human eyes, Hans wouldn't be able to make them out at this distance. But Gwen and Greta could see, hear, and smell him.

"You better be right, Rose Prospector," he muttered to himself, gently urging his spooked horse on, "and they come to talk to me, not eat me."

Greta looked at Gwen.

"Greta!" His tremulous voice became louder as he drew closer. "If you're there, please come and help. Both of you. Rose needs you. Robyn, too."

Greta was about to take a step forward and make herself visible, but Gwen nudged her to stop. She narrowed her wolf's eyes and stayed where she was.

"Come out, wherever you are," he tried again. "He will kill her if you don't come."

Gwen pushed her claws into the grass. "Hans isn't lying," Greta said. "He may be devoted to his captain, but he is still my brother, and I know he isn't lying. He's not part of any Wolfmounter trap." Gwen cocked her head, considering this.

"Rose has sent him," Greta insisted. "You have to trust me, whether you like it or not." She didn't wait for Gwen to answer. She stepped out onto the dirt path and ran toward her brother. Gwen growled and sprinted behind her. With only two legs, Greta was bound to be slower, and Gwen needed for them to get inside as fast as possible. She nudged Greta running next to her, and nudged her again, waiting for her to catch a clue.

In a few minutes, they had covered the distance and sprinted past an open mouthed Hans and on through the village gates. Gwen was unsure whether Hans was open mouthed to see his sister still alive or because she was riding into the village on the back of a huge white wolf.

The villagers were so engrossed with their skirmishes Rose knew it was pointless calling out to them. Peter was slowly coming to his senses, but of no use to anyone at the moment. Hans was nowhere to be seen. That left Rose in the cage, and Robyn lying under the full weight of Hunter.

"Finally, my love," he whispered. "I never thought a stupid girl like you could give me so much trouble. Well, I suppose I can count on my dear little sister-in-law to fuck things up, too." He looked over his shoulder, his eyes slits of malice. "Don't you worry. We will have some fun later, dearest sister."

She shivered at the hatred in his stare. "Let me out!" she yelled and flung herself against the iron bars.

Hunter ignored her and turned his attention to Robyn lying trapped under him. "Come on, wake up, my lovely!" He slapped her across the face. "Wakey, wakey, my little ray of sunshine."

Robyn's puffy, encrusted eyelids opened to bloodshot slits. She spat into his face.

"Yes!" Rose crowed.

Hunter dragged a hand across his face, angrily rubbing the spit away. With his other hand, he lunged for Robyn's neck, intent on strangling the last breath from her. He'd barely made contact when a shadow fell over him.

From her cage, Rose's view was blocked by a huge, white, furry body. It growled. Rose couldn't believe her eyes. Gwen was here! Hans had succeeded in opening the gates!

The white wolf bowled Hunter away from Robyn as if he were a skittle. He rolled across the stage, an ungainly lump of red cape and wildly kicking boots, his face was ashen. In a leap the wolf had him cowering under her, her fangs inches from his throat. A string of saliva oozed onto his pale cheek. Rose watched with bated breath, wondering at the hesitation, wishing Gwen would rip his throat out at once. *Kill him!*

But Gwen just held him pinned. Her head moved slightly, and Rose saw Gwen was distracted by Robyn. The girl lay unmoving as if her last act of anger against Hunter had used the last of her meager energy. The muscles in Gwen's broad shoulders softened momentarily. Rose's keen senses could pick up on the wolf's worry and confusion for her mate's well-being. She was torn between revenge and the need to help. Rose tensed. Gwen's distraction was obvious, even to Hunter, and she knew he would take advantage of this lapse. She prayed Gwen would come to her senses and end things before Hunter got a chance to act.

Robyn stirred, and made a small cry of pain. Immediately, the wolf swung her full attention onto her wounded mate.

Hunter slipped the knife from his boot top and plunged the short blade up to the hilt in the wolf's side.

There was a scream, and it took Rose a second to realize it was her own. The huge wolf staggered, and Hunter scrambled out from under her and lurched to his feet. He spun around half crouched, wildly slicing his knife through the air before him. His eyes were huge with fear in his chalk white face. Gwen snarled, her side was slick with crimson and Rose saw the slight tremor in her hind quarters as she stumbled backward. She managed to steady herself, backed up into a crouch, ready to lunge. Even though Rose could see she had been hurt, she seemed uncaring for the knife. Between the smell of Gwen's fresh blood and Robyn's stale, bruised flesh, Rose could make out another, new odor. Urine. The stain ran across Hunter's breeches and down his leg to disappear into the top of his right boot. He stood pissing himself with fear as Gwen leaped.

Man and wolf fell backward. Hunter screamed high and shrill. Rose saw his blade flash as he crumpled under the weight of the huge beast. The wolf lunged out, but Hunter trashed so wildly that she didn't manage to push the knife out of his hand. Instead, her claws scratched his shoulder. He screamed again, in an unnatural girlish shriek. One leg was pinned under the wolf's hindquarters, and with his other he kicked blindly at her. When Gwen yelped in pain, Rose knew Hunter had hit the wound on her side. The big wolf tumbled backward. His knife still in his hand, Hunter rolled onto his stomach, crawling on knees and elbows back to the unconscious Robyn.

"Gwen!" Rose yelled, but the wolf was even faster. She snarled and snatched at Hunter's leg to pull him back from her mate. With a wild and fearful roar he lashed out with the knife, but the wolf was out of reach. The square became still as everyone stopped in their tracks to watch. Awe and terror mixed on the upturned faces of the villagers. Even Hunter's Riders stood transfixed.

The wolf had him in her maw and shook him like a rag doll, as he screamed and kicked helplessly.

"Stop it!" came a yell. "Stop it at once!"

Rose turned to see Hans and Greta Sweets side by side, aiming their bows with arrows at Hunter and Gwen. They stood before Robyn, shielding her. Their faces were hard and grim.

"Hans. Hans, help me." The relief in Hunter's voice was tangible.

"Put the knife down, Wolfmounter," Hans said in a voice full of command and ice.

Hunter blinked stupidly. Gwen stepped back, but clumsily. The blood from her pelt now dripped onto the wood of the stage, mixing with Hunter's. Freed from the fangs Hunter scrambled to his knees.

"The knife!" Greta motioned with her bow, aiming right between Hunter's eyes. It skittered from his limp fingers onto the bloodied platform. He sat slumped on his heels, head hanging and chest heaving. Hans lowered his bow and turned to the crowd.

"This madness will stop. You will all come to order." His voice had an immediate effect. People became aware of where they were and what they had done. Peter was coming to his feet slowly, aided by Ash and Goldie. The Red Riders stood up straighter. What was left of their capes lay shredded around their feet. Everyone looked vaguely ashamed.

With all attention on Hans, Rose was the only one aware of Hunters hand slyly moving for the knife again. At least she thought she was the only one to notice. The wolf snarled, and with one great heave flung its wounded, bloody body at Hunter, throwing them both over the edge of the stage to the cobbles below and out of Rose's sight. The crowd screamed and scrambled back. Greta ran to the edge of the stage and raised her bow. She took careful aim at the skirmish below and fired.

Chapter 17

Robyn didn't want to open her eyes. With awakening came pain and worry, and maybe even loss. She knew she could cope with pain, but she couldn't cope with loss.

"Gwen?" She tried to yell but heard only the faintest whisper.

"I'm here." Gwen's voice was a balm to every ache in her heart and body. Opening her eyes would be worth it now. Gwen leaned over her, her gaze full of concern and love.

"How are you?" Robyn managed to rasp out the question. Her throat was unbearably dry. She hoped her weak smile would make the wrinkle on Gwen's forehead go away. It didn't. The wrinkle deepened to a frown. Gwen placed a glass of water to her lips, and she sipped gratefully.

"Don't ask me that, silly girl." Gwen brushed her lips over Robyn's cheek. "I thought I'd lost you. Three days of pacing up and down, knowing nothing, hardly sensing you. Don't ever—"

"I won't," Robyn said. She placed her hand on Gwen's and immediately felt a comfort in the heat of her skin. "What happened?"

Gwen nodded to the other side of the bed, and Robyn carefully turned her aching head to find Rose grinning down at her with tears in her eyes.

"It took us two days to clean you up and make you look half human." She laughed at her feeble, self-conscious joke.

"Aside from the little problem of your being caught and nearly dying on us, the plan worked well," Greta spoke softly from the foot of the bed. "Gwen has done a great job, and most of the girls are progressing nicely. They stood up for you, you know, in the market square. They resisted the Riders and, more importantly, ignored Hunter's orders."

"Not only the women." Gwen's voice was gruff enough for all of them to pay attention. She threw a look across the room to where Hans Sweets stood, highly embarrassed and looking at his shining boots. "We had unexpected allies." That was the most praise she could muster.

"Hunter?" Robyn asked.

Gwen's eyes darkened, and Robyn held her tight so she couldn't pull her hand away.

"He's sitting in the cage in the market square," Rose said proudly.

Robyn sighed; relief and pain whistled through her aching lungs. "So it's almost done."

"Almost," Gwen said and squeezed her fingers. "But we'll wait for you to get stronger. Now rest. I will stay here by your side."

Robyn thanked her friends for being there, and for caring, before she closed her eyes and drifted away to a more peaceful place. The last thought to float idly through her mind was why was Gwen wearing Hans Sweets' clothes?

It took another week for Robyn to be strong enough to walk unaided out to the market square. Gwen had gone back to the cabin and retrieved clothes for both of them. So now they stood on the stage across from the cage in well-fitting trousers and loose linen shirts. The square had returned to order from the previous scenes of civil unrest, where stones had shattered windows and carts had been overturned. The whole village was present, waiting for one person to speak.

Rose stepped forward. Her red cape snapped in the wind and matched the tone of her voice. Rose knew what she needed to say and was crisp, curt, and to the point. "As the new Captain of the Red Riders it is my duty to explain what lies ahead of us," she began and motioned for Greta to join her at her side. "Greta will make sure that all mature men, who have failed assessment, will leave before midnight. Those who have been claimed by a female family member may remain under village jurisdiction, but only for as long as they are endorsed by that same female family member."

About a hundred men stood lined up with their wagons, horses, and enough livestock to allow them to start a new life far, far away. They muttered and moaned in protest, but dared not raise their voices too loud. The past week had been a bitter experience for them as they were cast aside and disinherited by the new order that had invaded the village. The few who had survived the cull stood to one side of the square casting hard-eyed glares at their disenfranchised brethren.

Whitney Wolfmounter stepped forward. She clasped a hand to her pregnant belly and spoke up like a well-practiced martyr, "Since I wasn't allowed to vouch for him, I will leave with my husband."

Greta shook her head. "I'm sorry, but you do not want to walk the road Hunter Wolfmounter is about to travel."

"Rose!" Whitney turned wide-eyed to her sister. "Do something!"

Rose's gaze wandered down Whitney's leg to the bite mark. She gave a sorrowful frown. She shrugged. "I tried, but it didn't work," she said to no one in particular.

Whitney's tear-streaked face was red with anger. "Hunter was so good to you, how dare you betray his trust?" Her eyes wandered over the men prepared to leave and stopped at her father's huddled frame. "I use my right to vouch for Darwin Prospector, my dear father!"

Again Rose shook her head. "Dear sister, the voting is done. These men will go."

"Well, then," Whitney said, with as much dignity as she could muster. "I will go with our father rather than live in a world where a man and his wisdom are so despised. Man was created to tell us what to do. You women are all unnatural! And I for one, do not want my son growing up in a world where he'll not be master, so there."

She grabbed her bundle of belongings and waddled off to join her father in the wagon train heading out of the village. Granny shuffled forward and held onto her elbow. "Come child, I will go with you and tend to your baby boy and tell him about the great days, where men fought beasts and women took pleasure in serving them."

"The beasts or the men?" a woman's voice jeered from the back of the crowd.

"I wish you all a pleasant journey and hope never to see any of you ever again. Do not come near this village. And if any of you should return, our Red Riders will strike you down," Rose spoke again, looking from Greta to Robyn and Gwen. "Believe me, we will. You are all officially outcast."

There was more discontented grumbling from the outcasts, but again it didn't get too loud. Fear of the new Red Riders had already set in. Rose nodded to Greta, giving her a little smile.

Greta went over to the cage guarded by Hans and Peter, who were still part of the Riders though the troop was now almost entirely female. Hans opened the cage door. Peter offered her the rope tied around Hunter's neck. She took it carefully, not wanting to abuse his punished body even more. It was not hers to wound.

Hunter was a shell of a man, or maybe his true self was finally visible now that his gusto and hubris had been stripped away. He rose to his feet unsteadily and was pulled reluctantly from the cage. In the past few days, it was apparent the cage had become a refuge for him. He was resistant to emerge from it into the world he used to strut about and command so easily. The crowd hushed as Greta strode across the stage with him meekly following. Even the men excommunicated from their homes fell silent. Their eyes revealing how lucky they felt at that moment. At least they had a future to forge, the man who had led them to this desolation would have nothing.

Greta halted before Gwen and handed over the tether. Robyn stood silently by her lover's side. The wind blew chill, but she refused to shiver. This was both justice and revenge for Morganne, and it had taken a long time coming. Now that it was here words had no meaning.

"Gwen, the women of this village thank you for what you have done to help them," Greta said. "Herewith, I fulfill my promise to you. I can't turn back time, but I can help avenge the woman you loved."

Hunter seemed to break out of his stupor and lurched backward. Whatever punishment he had expected, it certainly hadn't been to be left at Gwen's mercy. The rope strained, and Gwen's grip on it tightened until he stilled. Then, like a cow led to the slaughter, he suddenly realized there was nowhere to go, no escape available, and no rescue coming. Hans and Peter stood either side of Greta stoically, and his Riders in the square below with carts packed and devoid of their red capes looked away mortified.

"Come," Gwen said simply, her voice emotionless. Only Robyn saw the faint quiver of her lip as she pulled Hunter away by the rope around his neck. They moved through the market square toward the North gate. The crowd parted for them, silent and sober. Gwen stopped and pushed him forward, so Hunter was walking in front of her now, the rope dangling loose over his shoulder. His hands weren't even bound, and still he walked on, finally accepting that there was no other fate than this one; the one he had made for himself so many years ago.

Epilogue

"Congratulations to us all." Robyn raised her glass to Ebony and Ash, who stood at the far end of the bar in Spindlefinger's inn. Goldie had kept the name because she still was a Spindlefinger, and the changes inside were more important to her than a name. But she had thrown her spinning wheel onto the trash heap. She had also turned the whole inn into a place of comfort and cleanliness. People came from all over to eat at the new Spindlefinger's. Her cooking was so fabulous that she already had converted her old market wagon to a movable diner and sold her wares at all the surrounding village markets. It turned out Goldie was even better at business than her penny-pinching ex-husband.

But they weren't celebrating Goldie's new wealth this evening. It had taken them many a month to get everything ready, and now it was finally time for Gwen and Robyn to get back home.

"When will the first children come?" Greta asked, taking a sip of her ale. Her cheeks shone rosily with the strength of it.

"Give it three more days and we will holler them all in," Ebony said, looking proudly over at Ash. With a little help from their friends, they had converted Ebony's father's house into a training center for girls. There they would learn to read and write, to cook if they wanted to, and calculus whether they wanted to or not. Once a week Peter had agreed to give them lessons in self-defense, and some of the other Riders, male and female, would be teaching riding, archery, and stable duties.

The glass factory was female-owned and managed, now. Even the burnt down stables were almost as good as new. They were slowly rebuilding the village into a place they wanted to live, and were proud to call home.

"Hey, a penny for your thoughts?" Gwen was by her side, nudging her shoulder.

"I'd prefer ale," she teased back.

"Hey, you two!" Rose squeezed in between them, hugging both their shoulders. She had not stopped smiling since Robyn had opened her eyes and declared herself healthy, and she didn't intend to stop anytime soon from the look of it. "I'm glad you decided to stay for the festivities so I can thank you properly, yet again."

"There is no need," Robyn said. It was an ongoing conversation. Rose needed to stop alternating her apologies with her thanks.

"Oh yes, there is." Rose insisted. "It would have never worked without you, and look what we've accomplished. We have finally broken free from the chains of men. Do you see all these women making plans of their own, not afraid to speak their minds? That is because of you two. Now we can work confidently and happily toward our future. It turns out we don't need anyone telling us what to do. We can make a better life for ourselves."

Robyn hugged Rose back, overwhelmed by her sheer happiness.

"Let the men be men, and let me hug you both one last time," Rose said, pulling them towards her. "And then I promise to stop grinning at you like an idiot."

They both hugged her, but it was Hans who saved them from her enthusiasm when he came over and asked her to dance.

Gwen raised an eyebrow as they spun off around the floor, laughing and talking, and bumping into other dancing couples.

Robyn shrugged. "He has always liked her, despite the difficulties. And she was the one who got him out from under Hunter's influence."

At the thought of Hunter, she still felt a light stab in her belly, though not for herself, but for Gwen. Gwen drank her ale steadily. She had come back from the woods alone, not bloody, not disheveled, nothing. And she had never talked about what happened. Hunter was dead, that was the only thing Robyn was sure of.

Greta watched Rose and Hans cavorting and shrugged. "It's about time Rose has some fun. He was never a bad brother. He just..."

"Was a weak-minded man," Gwen finished for her.

"In the end he stood beside us for the cause," Robyn reminded them both.

"I still like Peter better," Gwen mumbled, the wolf in her probably thankful for the cold compress to her wounds. Peter had taken care of her on the cobblestones of the market square while ignoring the whimpering of his captain with Greta's arrow sticking out of his leg. The boy was well on his way to being a kind and capable man who viewed all as equal, be they man, woman, or beast. His offer to cart food and supplies back to Gwen's cabin had been met with grudging agreement. It seemed the wily old wolf who was slow to trust, was partway to trusting him. Though he only got to leave the supplies several miles from the cabin, where Gwen could collect them. She didn't want to sniff any human scent so close to their home.

"It's time," she said, putting her hand on the small of Robyn's back. Greta gave them a sad smile, then motioned for Rose to come and join them outside.

The four of them stood and enjoyed the mild spring breeze and the promise of the new year it brought with it. No one spoke for a long while.

Rose was the first to break the silence. "Be careful out there, you never know what awaits you in the woods." She hugged Robyn tightly, one last time. "I'm glad I found you again," she whispered.

Robyn kissed her cheek. "You're a true friend, Rose. We'll meet again soon."

Greta extended her hand to Gwen; they had found a tentative peace around each other. Gwen still didn't trust Greta, in the long run, the loss of Morganne was too deep a wound to bridge. But she had made great efforts to see past her grudges and work alongside her as one of the new leaders of the village. And as a token of that growing trust Gwen and Robyn had agreed to patrol the woods around the village.

"Farewell, my friends," she said. "Be happy out there, and take good care of each other."

"We will," Gwen said, and Robyn hugged Greta goodbye.

They left through the North gate, hearing the laughter and joy spilling out from the inn until the heavy wooden gate closed behind them.

"Gwen?"

"Hmm?"

"We shall never part again."

Gwen rolled her eyes. "Aw, lass, don't get all sappy now."

"I'll show you sappy!" She pushed Gwen onto the wet grass, flinging herself on top of the bigger woman. Before Gwen could protest, Robyn plastered her face with wet kisses.

"Stop it, you little…" Gwen tried to turn her face away, but she couldn't win. And before Robyn could pull out of reach, Gwen had cradled her face and was pulling her down into a real, deep kiss, involving lots of tongue and lips, and even some teeth. Robyn felt herself blush, and tried to stand up so they could head to the cabin faster. They hadn't been alone since the day their plan had started, and she was eager for their own bed.

Gwen gave her a seductive smile. "It's a long way home, lass."

"Any suggestions?" Robyn teased, feeling the fire inside her rise.

Gwen grew serious and knelt in front of her. "Would you change for me?" she asked then, looking at Robyn expectantly.

"Always," Robyn said with a smile and began to run, for it was easier to become the wolf when in motion.

Behind her, she heard Gwen howl at the night sky, and felt the vibration of her approach through the wet earth up through her paws.

Robyn howled in return, feeling the joy pounding through her body. The village was taken care of, the minds of the women were free, *she* was free, and she had found love in a place where beasts weren't men, but men were beasts. And if this were a real fairy tale, then Robyn truly believed they would all live happily ever after.

About Nino Delia

Nino was born 1988 in the far north of Germany, whence she went out into the world to study literature. She earned a master's degree in Comparative Studies and now works, like every good arts scholar should once in his life, as a specialist for envelopes, staplers, and double-paged printed papers.

Nino doesn't like to be limited. On the contrary: She writes whatever catches her interest.

She likes word games, dark stories, and biting humor. She sympathizes mostly with the underdog instead of the shining hero.

CONNECT WITH NINO:
Website: http://ninodelia.wordpress.com
Facebook: http://www.facebook.com/ninodelia1
E-mail: nino.delia@aol.de

Other Books From Ylva Publishing

www.ylva-publishing.com

Banshee's Honor

Shaylynn Rose

ISBN: 978-3-95533-103-0

Warleader. This is what the people of Y'Dan used to call the proud warrior Azhani Rhu'len.

Banshee. Oath breaker. Murderer. These are words that slip off their tongues now.

Azhani Rhu'len, once one of the greatest of Y'Dan's warriors, is now just a common criminal, escaping the justice of the kingdom she swore to serve.

~~~

Kyrian Stardancer. Goddess' Own. A healer and priestess, she is inviolate until one day, when her world is turned upside down and tossed over the back of a horse—literally.

Torn from all she knows, Kyrian finds her fate now rests squarely on the shoulders of the oath breaker, Azhani Rhu'len.

When signs of ancient evil appear, Azhani and Kyrian must choose whether to ignore the warnings or stand and face the terrifying menace.
~~~

Sigil Fire

Erzabet Bishop

ISBN: 978-3-95533-206-8

Sonia is a succubus with one goal: stay off Hell's radar. But when succubi start to die she's drawn into battle between good and evil.

Fae is a blood witch turned vampire, running a tattoo parlor and trading her craft for blood. She notices that something isn't right on the streets of her city. The denizens of Hell are restless.

The killer has a target in sight, and Sonia might not survive.

Coming From Ylva Publishing In 2015

www.ylva-publishing.com

Banshee's Vengeance

Shaylynn Rose

Honor. It was torn from Azhani's grasp by the sorcerer whose hatred of her family is decades old.

Love. Ylera, Azhani's beloved, was murdered, her death no more than one callous act in a chain meant to put a noose around Azhani's neck.

Once, not long ago, Azhani had been hopeless, lost, and without any desire for a future, but now, the rimerbeasts have come, and she is needed. Can she put aside her yearning for justice and face this ancient menace as honor demands, or will the bonds of love lost hurl her into a mire of death and revenge?

The Tea Machine

Gill McKnight

The story of a love that never dies...except it does, over and over again.

London 1862, and Millicent Aberly, spinster by choice, has found her future love—in the future! She meddled with her brother's time machine and has been catapulted into an alternative world where the Roman Empire has neither declined nor fell. In fact, it has gone on to annex most of the known universe.

Millicent is rescued from Rome's greatest enemy, the giant space squid, by Sangfroid, a tough and wily centurion who, unfortunately, dies while protecting her. Wracked by guilt and a peculiar fascination for the woman soldier, Millicent is determined to return in time and save Sangfroid from her fatal heroics. Instead, she finds her sexy centurion in her own timeline. And Sangfroid is not alone; several stowaways have come along with her.

Soon Millicent's mews house is overrun with Roman space warriors and giant squid.

The Secret of Sleepy Hollow

Andi Marquette

Tabitha "Abby" Crane, a doctoral student working on her thesis, doesn't allow herself much time outside academia. Fortunately, she's managed to squeeze in a research trip over Halloween weekend to the historical society of Sleepy Hollow, New York, where she hopes to uncover new research on the notorious town's most infamous legend—that of the headless horseman. But she has a personal stake in this trip: Abby's own ancestor, Ichabod Crane, disappeared mysteriously over two hundred years ago, perhaps at the hands of the ghostly horseman.

Abby has no reason to expect anything of Sleepy Hollow beyond immersing herself in archival collections and enjoying its Halloween festivities, but then she crosses paths with Katie, who makes her head spin and her heart pound. When Katie invites her on a nighttime visit to the glen where the horseman allegedly rides, Abby can't say no, upending her plans for a quiet research retreat. And when Abby and Katie, who has her own ties to the famous story, find what may be the key to the disappearance of Ichabod Crane all those years ago, love, legend, and magic intermingle, making clear that Sleepy Hollow has plans of its own for yet another Crane.

Caged Bird Rising. A Grim Tale of Women, Wolves, and other Beasts
Nino Delia

ISBN: 978-3-95533-319-5

Also available as e-book.

Published by Ylva Publishing, legal entity of Ylva Verlag, e.Kfr.

Ylva Verlag, e.Kfr.
Owner: Astrid Ohletz
Am Kirschgarten 2
65830 Kriftel
Germany

www.ylva-publishing.com

First Edition: August 2015

Credits:
Edited by Gillian A. McKnight
Proofread by Blythe Rippon
Cover Design by Streetlight Graphics

This book is a work of fiction. Names, characters, events, and locations are fictitious or are used fictitiously. Any resemblance to actual persons or events, living or dead, is entirely coincidental.

Lightning Source UK Ltd.
Milton Keynes UK
UKOW01f1905100416

271930UK00001B/11/P